Praise for *Their One and Only*
Written by Trista Ann Michaels

"*Their One and Only* is a terrific read for anyone who is looking for a love story with a little drama and a lot of heart."

—*Literary Nymphs*

"An intelligent, yet seductive tale from the pen of Trista Ann Michaels, *Their One and Only* is a powerful love story not to be missed."

—Courtney Michelle, *Romance Reviews Today*

"*Their One and Only* was a wonderful, fast paced story that I wasn't able to put down. If you like a mystery with some hot sex thrown in this is definitely the one for you."

—Julia, *The Romance Studio*

"Trista Ann Michaels is definitely a gifted writer and *Their One and Only* was pure erotic magic. The story flowed so well that it had me reading from start to finish in one sitting. This is definitely a must own novel."

—Kimberly Spinney, *eCataRomance*

D0187935

LooseId®

ISBN 10: 1-59632-753-7
ISBN 13: 978-1-59632-753-5
THEIR ONE AND ONLY
Copyright © July 2008 by Trista Ann Michaels
Originally released in e-book format in January 2008

Cover Art by Christine M. Griffin
Cover Layout by April Martinez

DISCLAIMER: Many of the acts described in our BDSM/fetish titles can be dangerous. Please do not try any new sexual practice, whether it be fire, rope, or whip play, without the guidance of an experienced practitioner. Neither Loose Id nor its authors will be responsible for any loss, harm, injury or death resulting from use of the information contained in any of its titles.

This book is an original publication of Loose Id. Each individual story herein was previously published in e-book format only by Loose Id and is a work of fiction. Any similarity to actual persons, events or existing locations is entirely coincidental.

Printed in the U.S.A. by
Lightning Source, Inc.
1246 Heil Quaker Blvd
La Vergne TN 37086
www.lightningsource.com

THEIR ONE AND ONLY

Trista Ann Michaels

Chapter One

"Perfect. Now turn that way, toward my assistant, and smile for me."

Kaycee Alcott turned toward Murphy and smiled softly. Murphy grinned back, almost making her giggle with the goofy-looking faces he kept shooting her way. This was her fifth photo shoot with Jean Claude, and she knew what he wanted as far as a smile.

As a top photographer in the modeling world, he photographed huge names, but for this project, he'd specifically asked for her, which made her all the more determined to do her best. The last thing she wanted to do was disappoint Jean Claude.

"Let me see a little more of that gorgeous thigh, Kaycee," he said, and she used her hand to slide the split in the skirt further to the side. "Perfect."

The camera kept clicking, the sound barely heard over Jean Claude's orders about lighting and wind position. She was thankful for the fan as it blew a soft breeze in her face, cooling the flesh the lights warmed up. A photography studio could be as much as twenty degrees hotter than anywhere else because of all the equipment.

Jean Claude stopped and spread his arms wide, smiling from ear to ear. "Beautiful as always, Kaycee," he purred in a soft French accent. "We're all done."

"Already?" she asked in surprise, then glanced down at the pink sundress she'd worn for the shoot. "I couldn't by any chance sneak this out, could I?" She glanced at him through her lashes.

"I did not see a thing," he said, fiddling with his camera. "She wore her coat when she left. How was I to know what was under it?"

Kaycee laughed and ran over to place a quick kiss on his cheek. "You're a riot, Jean Claude. Thank you," she added in a soft whisper.

He smiled, his green eyes crinkling at the corners and showing his advanced age. "You did an amazing job, as always. As far as I'm concerned, you deserve the dress."

Giving him her best grin, she turned and headed to the dressing area to gather her things. It wasn't unusual for models to take things from shoots. Some designers even expected it. At the makeup counter, she sat in the chair and reached for a moist cloth to clean her face. She'd sent her assistant home over an hour ago, since the shoot had taken place so late. No sense in both of them being bleary-eyed for the runway rehearsal tomorrow morning.

With a tired sigh, Kaycee wiped away the mascara and dark lipstick, then brushed out her dark brown curls, securing them on top of her head with a scrunchie. Now that the shoot was over, fatigue began to sink in. Her bed was what she needed. That and about fifteen hours of uninterrupted sleep.

She'd never thought about being a model until an agent from Sloan Modeling approached her at a coffee shop just off the NYU campus. She'd been nineteen and skeptical.

At first, the shoots had been a way to pay for her college tuition, but then assignments began to come in so fast, she hadn't been able to keep up with her classes and had to drop out her senior year. She had enough money invested now, she could quit modeling and go back to school if she wanted. The only problem was, she didn't know what she wanted to do anymore.

"No doubt about it," she murmured, giving herself one final look in the mirror to make sure she'd gotten all the makeup. "I'm definitely in a funk."

Standing, she slid her arms into her coat and prepared to go out into the cold parking garage. Her fingers brushed over her scarf, and a sad smile tugged at her lips. The scarf had been her father's -- the only thing she had left of him -- and she never went anywhere cold without it.

With a tired sigh, she wrapped the scarf round her neck. *There's no point in thinking about the past and what should have been.* She was on her own now, except for her best friend and assistant, and she needed to accept it.

She grabbed her overnight bag, stuffed with her clothes from earlier, her makeup, and her hair rollers, and headed out of the studio. "Good night, guys," she called as she walked past Jean Claude and his assistants.

"Do you want me to walk out with you?" Jean Claude asked.

She shook her head. "No. I'll be fine."

"All right," he said and waved. "Good night, then. I'll send you a set of the proofs."

"Thanks, Jean Claude," she replied with a smile. "You're the best."

"Of course, I am," he teased. "That's why I get the best girls."

He winked and she laughed as she pushed the door open with her hip. A cold blast of air hit her as she walked across the parking lot toward her car, a sunburnt orange Chevy HHR. She'd tried to be smart about her money, investing most of it for when modeling was no longer an option. She didn't need the flashy car or the huge house. Security was more her thing -- financial security for her future.

The cold night sky was clear, the stars sparkling above her like twinkling lights. Stopping at her car, she took a moment to breathe in the fresh winter air and admire the horizon.

A sharp pain in her thigh made her gasp, and she turned to see a man looming over her. Fear tightened her chest as he held up a needle, his eyes shining in triumphant glee. She raised her hand to shove him away, but her limbs felt heavy and her hand tangled in the wool of her scarf. In confusion, she tugged, making it fall to the concrete.

Her heart should have been hammering, but it seemed to slow, along with her thoughts. Fatigue deepened as the warmth of the drug spread through her body. No. She couldn't let this happen. She couldn't let him do this.

Taking a step forward, she latched on to his black coat as her legs wobbled beneath her. He just stood there, watching her with dark eyes full of hatred and loathing. Why would he hate her? She squinted, narrowing her gaze on the wool covering his face. She tried to lift her other hand as her vision blurred even more. Time moved in slow motion as her body took on the consistency of concrete, unmovable and cold. Her heavy lids closed and she fell into a deep darkness, too numb to even be afraid.

He watched as Kaycee slowly slid to the ground, her fingers still clutching at his jacket. He'd waited months for this opportunity. She was a hard person to catch alone.

His cock twitched in his pants as he imagined all the things he'd do to her. All the other women had just been for fun, honing his skills, curbing his hunger until he caught his one true target.

Kaycee Alcott would pay for turning her back on him, for leading him on, then running like a scared rabbit the first time he tried to kiss her. His lip curled. He'd kiss her this time and a hell of a lot more.

* * *

"I'm glad the two of you could make it."

Sam and Tyler Warren both turned to Agent Barreck as he stepped into the small room and dropped a scarf on the table. Barreck had called them at four this morning, wanting their psychic input on a missing person's case. Sam and his identical twin, Tyler, had worked for the FBI as registered psychics for almost twenty years now, since they were twelve, and were responsible for solving over two hundred missing person's cases. According to Barreck, however, this was more than *just* a missing person. He believed this woman had been taken by their most elusive serial killer. A man they'd dubbed "the phantom".

Tyler and Sam had spent most of the last several months working a profile for this case. The phantom could get in, get a woman, and get out without being seen by anyone. He left no clues, no evidence. Even the bodies he'd left behind all over the eastern United States had been clean. He could pick a girl up in Myrtle Beach, and they would find her dead body in Kentucky. There was no pattern, no reason. The only thing the murders had in common were the girls' looks.

They were stumped, but Barreck believed they may have caught a break. The kidnapper had left behind a scarf.

"How do you know it's him?" Tyler asked as he turned to study a haggard-looking Barreck.

Barreck sighed and dropped into one of the leather conference chairs. "I don't. Truthfully, I'm just guessing. That's why I wanted you to take a look" -- he waved his hand -- "or whatever it is you do and see if it's his."

"Who reported her missing?" Sam asked.

"Her assistant." Barreck flipped through the file. "A Jordan Smith, when Kaycee didn't show up for runway rehearsal this morning. The photographer found her car right where she'd left it the night before."

"She's a model?" Tyler asked.

"Yes. Quite popular, from what I understand."

He pulled a photo from the file and passed it to Tyler. His gaze wandered over her china doll features and expressive emerald green eyes. She was definitely a beauty.

Raising his eyebrow, he passed the photo to his brother, who whistled softly.

"She certainly fits the image of the others he's taken. But isn't she a little too high profile for him?" Sam asked with a frown.

"She could be who he's been after all along," Tyler offered with a shrug, then stood to pour himself more coffee from the pot at the far side of the room.

"Well," Barreck said with a sigh. "You've always thought he had a particular girl in mind."

"They were too much alike. They either look like someone from his past or someone he wants."

Sam nodded and handed Tyler his cup to fill as well. "My guess would be it's someone he wants. He's strayed from the norm by taking someone as high profile as Kaycee."

"I agree," Tyler said.

Barreck leaned forward and wiggled the scarf still lying on the table. "We don't have a lot of time, guys. See if you can link up" -- he waved his hand again -- "or whatever it is you do to connect with the killer."

Sam snorted, then reached out to finger the wool. "High dollar," he murmured as he studied the worn scarf. "And old. Worn."

Tyler sat back down slowly, hesitant to touch it and actually see into the killer's mind. They'd connected with victims many times but with a serial killer only once, and the experience had left Tyler with a bad taste in his mouth. He didn't like what he'd seen, what he'd felt -- the darker side of human nature. Insanity was frightening, but even more frightening was just how coldly calculating the killer had been -- how cruel and angry.

Rubbing at his lips, Tyler sighed then met his brother's questioning gaze. He was sure Sam knew what fears held him in their grip. The two of them were like one person. They felt each other's fears, each other's conflicts. They even fell in love with the same women. If one loved a woman, then so did the other. It made dating difficult and the idea of marriage even more so.

"Tyler," Sam said softly. "You don't have to do this."

"No," Tyler replied, shaking his head. "We need to so we can find her."

Sam nodded and waited patiently for Tyler to touch the scarf as well. The link only worked if they were both touching it, but Tyler's connection went deeper than Sam's. Sam saw through the victims' eyes. Tyler could, as well, but he also felt what they felt. If they hurt, then so did Tyler.

Reaching out, Tyler placed his hand on the wool, bracing himself. But what he sensed surprised him. It wasn't anger. It was confusion. Fear.

"It's not his," Tyler whispered.

"What do you mean?" Barreck asked. "What are you seeing?"

Tyler closed his eyes, trying to focus. He felt sleepy and disoriented. She'd been drugged and was having difficulty waking up. "It's hers and she's still alive."

* * *

Kaycee struggled to sit up. Grogginess fuddled her mind, kept her from remembering. Had she wrecked her car? She certainly felt like she had. Every part of her ached as though she'd been beaten. Her leg burned like she'd been stung by a bee, and her muscles felt weak and drained.

She tried to raise her hand to wipe at her eyes, but couldn't. She tried the other one, but it, too, wouldn't move but just a few scant inches. *What?* Her heart skipped in her chest as she tugged at the bindings holding her down. Opening her eyes, she stared at the rope holding her wrists to the metal frame of the bed. She blinked, trying to clear the blurry images and remember what happened.

There'd been a man. He'd drugged her with something.

Shaking her head, she tugged at the ropes again, to no avail. Real fear began to settle in her chest as she glanced around the darkened room, her eyes still not fully able to focus. She scooted down along the table, adjusting her body to reach the knot at her wrist with her teeth. Cold air drifted across her naked flesh, making her shiver and her fingers tremble. Her jaw ached as she tugged at the knots, the dirty taste of the rope filling her mouth.

A noise to her right made her freeze, her breath lodging in her throat. Raising her gaze, she searched the dark, damp room. Was there someone here with her? Beside the table on which she was strapped was another table. A light hung over it, illuminating an empty white sheet. She gasped as she noticed the dried blood covering the material, the stainless steel surgical instruments lying on a portable tray at the foot.

Oh, my God.

She continued to scan the room, her gaze taking in everything. It actually wasn't a room. It was a cave with rock walls and damp floors. A dark opening was to her left, but she couldn't see past it. It appeared to only lead into darkness, but it had to be a way out.

"This is insane," she whispered, still in shock and disbelief.

She knew how to protect herself, so how had this guy managed to sneak up on her?

"I have to find a way out." She continued to scan the cave, looking for a possible way out and whomever had made the noise.

Against the far wall rested a pegboard covered in pictures of a woman. Kaycee swallowed down the bile that threatened to choke her as the pictures slowly came into focus.

Oh, my God. Those are me.

Every one of the pictures was of her. Snapshots of her around New York and Boston. There were several of her magazine covers and ads. She swallowed down the hysteria threatening to consume her. Whoever this man was, he'd been following her. Stalking her.

The noise again caught her attention, and she quickly looked around, squinting into the dark corners. "Who's there?" she demanded, her voice harsh and raw.

"Please." A woman whimpered, and Kaycee turned her head to the left.

Against the wall, chained in irons, lay a young woman, her hair a matted mess, her eyes glazed over, her face swollen and bloody. Deep cuts and bruises covered her naked flesh, bringing tears to Kaycee's eyes.

"Are you okay?" Kaycee asked. "Can you hear me?"

"I'm next," the girl murmured, her words barely audible.

"What? What do you mean?" Kaycee resumed tugging at the ropes on her left wrist with her teeth, her gaze never leaving the young woman.

"When he brings a new girl in, he kills the old one. He killed the last one in front of me."

Kaycee stopped tugging at the ropes and stared in shock. "He does what?"

"Now that you're here, he'll kill me. He'll use my body to show you what he'll do to you. And he'll do it," she slurred, her eyes falling closed.

"Wait, wait. No, stay with me," Kaycee demanded. "What's your name?"

"Miranda."

"I'm Kaycee. And I'm going to get us out of here."

"I can't walk." Miranda nodded to her oddly bent ankles.

Kaycee gasped at the girl's swollen feet and lower legs. "I'll help you out," she said with more confidence than she felt. "Who is he?"

"I don't know. I've never seen his face. He keeps it hidden."

Fear gave her strength, determination as she worked frantically at the bindings biting into her flesh. Her wrists were raw and sore; the smell of blood and death began to fill her nostrils, and she tried to breathe more through her mouth. She had to get out of here. She refused to die like this.

Finally the knot loosened and she giggled, out of her mind now from fear. "I've almost got it," she murmured, then glanced over at Miranda. Her eyes were closed, her breathing shallow and harsh.

Oh, God, please let me get us out of here.

With one final tug, she loosened the ropes enough to slip her wrist out. With her free hand, she began to loosen the other set of ropes around her right arm. Her fingers were shaking so badly she could hardly work them, and her lips had begun to tremble from the cold. After a few seconds, she was able to free her other hand, and with a sigh of relief, she sat up.

The cave spun off kilter, making her dizzy and nauseated. Leaning over the side of the table, she threw up what little was in her stomach. Dry heaves wracked her body for several seconds before she was able to get it under control. She sat back up, this time more slowly, allowing her stomach time to adjust. Whatever drug he'd given her had really done a number on her body.

She swung her legs to the side and set her bare feet on the ice-cold floor. She hissed as the cold shock worked its way up her legs, settling in her bones. Taking a deep breath, she fought off the second wave of nausea and stood. She took a step forward, then almost fell as the cave again began to spin. She reached out and placed her hand against the stone wall beside her to steady herself.

This was nuts. She'd never get herself out of here at this rate, much less both of them. She blinked, trying to focus her mind and keep the dizziness at bay. She had to get to Miranda.

Tyler gasped as the wave of nausea gripped him. Turning his head, he vomited in the trashcan close by, his hand holding tight to the scarf between him and his brother.

"You all right, Tyler?" Barreck asked, concerned. "What happened?"

"She's been drugged. She's sick." Tyler coughed, then spit into the can.

"You're sick because she's sick?" Barreck asked in surprise. "I've never seen you do that before."

"I was never this close to them before." Tyler sat back up, trying to numb his body to what she felt. "Stay with her, Sam," he whispered, and his brother nodded.

"She's free. She's trying to get to the other girl."

"There's another girl?" Barreck asked.

Tyler nodded, then closed his eyes, trying to recapture the images. "The other girl is chained up. Kaycee shouldn't do it."

"She's going to," Sam said.

"She's going to what?" Barreck asked in exasperation.

"She's going to try and get her out," Tyler said, shaking his head against the dizziness. "She'll never make it with her. The other girl is too hurt, and if Kaycee feels like I do, she can hardly walk."

"Where are they?"

Sam shook his head. "I can't tell. They're in a cave, but I have no way of knowing where."

Barreck slammed his hand on the table. "Damn it!"

Kaycee staggered toward Miranda. Her legs were so wobbly, so weak, she could hardly stand, but she had to do this. She couldn't leave Miranda behind. Kneeling by the other girl's side, Kaycee tugged at the iron bracelets around Miranda's wrists. The girl whimpered and shied away in fear.

"It's okay. I'm sorry. I'm so sorry. Your wrists, they're so badly cut and raw."

"That's the least of my pains," Miranda whispered.

Now that Kaycee was this close, she got a good look at Miranda's injuries. Several of her teeth were gone, her eyes were blood red and swollen, and her face was so badly contorted they would probably never be able to identify her. Tears slipped down Kaycee's cheeks as she renewed her struggle with the locks.

There had to be something somewhere. Standing, she slowly worked her way to the array of surgical instruments to find something she could use to pick the lock. Her hands were so shaky she knocked numerous things off the tray in her haste. More surgical instruments, more pictures. A fucking video camera? In anger she grabbed it and threw it against the wall. It shattered, falling to the floor in pieces. A sob broke from her chest as she struggled to keep from throwing up again.

"You're her," Miranda murmured.

"What?"

"The girl in the photos. Before he… I've had several people tell me I look like you. I guess he thought I did, too. He even called me Kaycee a few times."

Kaycee stared at her in shock. He'd been taking women that look like her?

"Oh, God," Miranda gasped. "He's coming."

A tremor of fear snaked down Kaycee's spine as she turned to stare at the cave opening. She could hear his footsteps as he made his way through the cavern toward the smaller room. She frantically searched for something to use as a weapon. Spotting the surgical knife, she made a move to grab it but knocked it off the table in her haste.

"Damn it," she hissed, unable to find it in the darkened room.

His footsteps were getting closer; she didn't have enough time to look for it. Glancing up, her eyes landed on a board about the size of a bat in the corner. She quickly grabbed it, then moved to the side of the opening, hoping he looked toward her table and Miranda first.

A tall form filled the opening, dressed in black, his face covered with the same ski mask as before. As for height, he wasn't much taller than her. Maybe an inch, if that. His shoulders were slightly wide, hinting at a little bit of strength, and she swallowed a lump of anxiety. Her fingers flexed around the board as she slowly raised it over her shoulder like a bat.

"Please, please, please," she chanted to herself, then swung with all her might.

He turned to face her just before the board hit him on the side of the head. With a grunt, he fell to the floor, motionless. She stood over him, her board ready to swing again, but he remained still, the only sound in the room her shallow breaths and Miranda's whimpers.

Fighting a rolling stomach and dizziness, she dropped the board and quickly searched the floor for the knife she'd dropped seconds before. She spotted it under the table and quickly grabbed it. She almost fell twice making her way back to Miranda and cursed at her clumsiness.

With a sob, she dropped to her knees and tried to work the lock free with the narrow knife. "Damn it," she sobbed. "I can't get it."

"Get out." Miranda moaned. "Please."

Kaycee shook her head. "No. I'm not going to leave you behind. I won't."

"I won't make it, and I'll only slow you down."

"No," Kaycee said firmly, glancing over her shoulder to make sure the man was still down.

"You can't carry me!" Miranda shouted. "You can barely walk yourself, and I can't walk at all."

Tears streamed down Kaycee's face as she shook her head in denial. There had to be a way. She refused to leave this girl behind to die.

"Kaycee," Miranda whispered, and she could tell by the tone of her voice something was wrong.

Turning slowly, she watched in growing fear as the man on the floor began to move. "Oh, my God." She again began to struggle with the bindings.

"Kaycee, please," Miranda pleaded. "Please get out."

"Not without you."

"Kaycee! Kaycee, he's coming!"

Kaycee spun around and frantically tried to think of what to do as he struggled to his knees.

"Get out!" Miranda shouted. "Please get out. You're our only hope."

"I can't leave you." She studied the surgical knife in her hand.

"Yes, you can. Please. You have to. If you don't get out, he'll kill us both," Miranda sobbed. "Please get help. Please."

Kaycee braced herself as the man rose slowly, his hand resting against his head. An angry growl rumbled through his chest, and she cringed.

"Please," Miranda whispered, and Kaycee stared at the knife in her hand.

Could she kill him? She'd never killed anyone, never imagined she'd be in a position that she would have to. She stood slowly, her free hand holding the wall to steady herself. The knife was small, narrow. Even if she were lucky enough to hit a vital spot, she was doubtful it would do enough damage to kill him. Her best chance would be his neck.

He turned slowly, his hand still against the side of his head. He saw her immediately and stiffened, anger flaring from the depths of his dark eyes. "You bitch," he snarled. "You'll pay for that."

She lowered her hand, trying to keep her weapon hidden as she waited for the right moment. If she struck too soon, he could block her and take the only weapon she had away from her. She took a step toward him, her gaze flicking to the entrance -- her only way out.

He stalked toward her, and she gasped at his speed. He was on her too quickly for her fogged mind to keep up. His hand landed across her cheek, sending her to the floor. Strobes of light flashed behind her eyes as she hit the hard ground, sending shards of pain through her limbs. Her fingers kept their grip on the knife as she glared up at him. Miranda cried in the background. Kaycee felt like crying, as well, but instead she let her anger take over.

With determination, she lunged upward, burying the knife in her attacker's stomach. Warm blood trickled over her fingers, and she let go of the handle as though she'd been burned, unable to stand the feel of it on her hands. He fell to his knees with a groan.

Standing on shaky legs, she kicked at her attacker's stomach, knocking him backward, his angry howls of pain drowning out Miranda's screams for her to run. Everything moved in slow motion as Kaycee struggled to get away, and she growled in frustration. Her legs felt rooted in concrete. She couldn't make them move fast enough.

Sobbing, she made her way to the entrance, not once looking back. She didn't have to. She could hear him shouting obscenities at her, warnings of all the things he would do to her.

"You'll hurt more than any of them, you bitch," he snarled.

"Fuck you," she screamed back.

Once inside the main corridor of the cave, she turned to her left, heading toward a sliver of light at the far end. *Please let this be a way out.* Her legs shook from the exertion. Her heart pounded so hard from fear she was certain it would jump from her chest. She could hear her attacker, smell him as he worked his way down the hall after her, screaming threats and obscenities the whole way.

She tripped over a rock. She reached down, gut instinct telling her to pick it up. A hand wrapped in her hair just as she reached the opening. She cried, screaming as he tugged her backward. Tears gathered in her eyes as she lost her balance and fell backward, despair weighing her down. Kicking her feet, she scraped the back of her heels along the ground, trying to fight her way back to a standing position. With a shock, she remembered the rock and swung it, hitting him just above the temple. He groaned and staggered back, letting go of her hair.

She twisted on all fours, not bothering to look back. With a cry, she lunged forward. Fear turned to adrenaline, giving her a second wind. With both hands forward, she burst through the thick layering of brush covering the opening, squinting as the bright sunlight hit her eyes.

"She's out," Sam said, and Tyler squinted with a wince as the bright light temporarily blinded him.

"Where is she?" Barreck asked. "Come on, guys. Give me something. Anything."

"We're trying, but…" Tyler shook his head, trying to clear his vision. "Sam, it's too bright. I can't see anything. She's so scared."

"She's in a forest. Lots of trees."

Tyler cringed as pain sliced through his feet. "God, she's running through the forest barefoot. The limbs on the ground, they're...they're cutting her feet."

Tyler couldn't breathe. Fear made his hands and legs shake, his heart pound. He'd never been this close to someone, this connected, and if he'd been able to think clearly, it would have terrified him. But they couldn't break the contact -- they couldn't let her go.

"You're too close to her," Sam said, and Tyler reached out to grip his wrist with his free hand.

"Don't you dare let go of that fucking scarf!"

Kaycee panted, tears streaming down her face as she made her way through the brush. Her arms and legs were bleeding, her breasts and stomach scratched. It was her feet that hurt the worst. Gashes on her soles sent searing pain up her legs with every step while the cold damp air gnawed at her nakedness and seeped into her bones like dull knives.

Her fingers and toes were numb, her lips shivering so hard her teeth rattled. Snow fell around her, clinging to the barren branches and fallen leaves, making the ground slippery.

She could hear him behind her, his steps, his grunts, and heavy breathing getting closer with every passing second. She had to find a way out of these trees. She had to find help.

Making a split-second decision to go right, she turned and ran, almost tripping over a log as the ground took a major slant downhill. With a squeal, she righted herself by grabbing on to a small tree. A piece of bark ripped her fingernail off, but she was so scared she barely noticed it. Instead, she kept her focus on the road below her about forty yards.

She took off as fast as her weak legs and injured feet would carry her. A car was coming over the hill, the sunlight shining on the blue lights on the roof. As she jumped the ditch next to the road, she prayed she wasn't hallucinating, prayed that really was a police car coming toward her. As her foot landed on the edge of the ditch, she fell, sprawling face first onto the concrete and almost directly in the path of the oncoming car. Tiny pebbles bit into her flesh, making her whimper in pain.

The car skidded to a halt, its tires squealing. She closed her eyes tightly, waiting for the crushing pain as the car ran over her battered body, too tired to move, too scared to scream. The car screeched to a stop just a few inches from her shoulder.

"Blount County Sheriff's Department," Sam said in relief. "She's one damn lucky woman."

Tyler let go of the scarf and drew in a deep breath to calm his rattled nerves. "Blount County." He sighed and let his head drop back. He had a serious headache pounding behind his eyes. "Where have I heard that?"

"It's where I go fly fishing," Sam said. "She's in Tennessee."

Barreck jumped up from his chair, reaching for the phone on the wall to call the Blount County Sheriff's Department.

"I want to go to Tennessee, Sam," Tyler said, thankful that his brother didn't give him any grief over getting too involved. Instead, he just nodded, silently agreeing.

Chapter Two

Kaycee awoke with a start, her eyes glancing anxiously about the dim room. A clamp closed over the tip of her index finger and hooked into a machine that read her heart rate. Oxygen blew into her nose through a small tube just above her lip. Sitting up, she winced as pain sliced through her muscles. Her bandaged feet burned and stung, her battered joints screamed in discomfort. Her gaze moved around the hospital room as her mind pieced together the events of the last two days.

Severe lacerations covered the bottom of both her feet. She'd lost one fingernail and suffered a black eye, twenty-four hours of vomiting from the drug he'd used on her, and a slight case of hypothermia. Her injuries seemed mild in comparison to the other girl in that cave with her.

"You shouldn't be sitting up just yet, Kaycee," a deep voice said from her left, and she turned to stare in surprise at the man coming to sit on the side of her bed.

His hands pushed at her shoulders, helping her to lie back down. Her stomach flipped as the man stared at her with heavenly royal blue eyes filled with concern surrounded by long black lashes and crinkling laugh lines. His face sported a thin layer of whiskers that surrounded full lips that looked as though they were made for kissing. Women would kill for lips like that. Despite how handsome he was, fear still raced through her.

"Who are you?" she asked, shrinking away from him. The machine beside her beeped faster as her pulse sped up from anxiety. Would she ever feel safe again?

"It's okay," he said. "I'm Tyler Warren." He pulled out his wallet and showed his badge.

"FBI?" she murmured.

"Yes. I'm the criminal profiler on your case."

"Profiler?" she asked skeptically, trying to ignore how his eyes sparkled. How the width of his shoulders dwarfed her.

He ran a strong hand through his hair. "Yeah. I've been helping track down the man that took you."

"Did you get him?"

"I'm afraid not," he said softly.

Her hands began to shake as fear once again knotted her stomach. "He's still out there?"

"It's going to be okay." His warm hands covered hers, but the thought of a man touching her right now made her flinch and she jerked her hand away. "My brother and I won't let anything happen to you, I promise."

"Did they find Miranda?" she asked. He looked down at the floor, avoiding her gaze, and her lower lip began to tremble in dread. He wouldn't even look at her. She knew what that meant. "No," she whispered. "Oh, no."

"I'm sorry, Kaycee. When we finally found where you'd been, he'd already killed her."

Kaycee covered her mouth with her hand, choking back a sob. Regret slammed her chest with the force of a wrecking ball. "No." She shook her head, tears streaming down her face. "I shouldn't have left her."

"It's not your fault, Kaycee." His hands cupped her cheeks, forcing her head up. "Look at me. You did the right thing."

"Leaving her was not the right thing," she snapped.

"If you hadn't you would both be dead. Is that what you wanted? For him to kill both of you?"

Kaycee choked back a sob and shook her head.

"You made it out."

"But I can't identify him. He kept his face covered the whole time. For all I know it could have been you," she cried. "What good can I do now? She should have never died. I should have fought harder to get her out."

"Kaycee," Tyler said, brushing her hair from her face. "Don't do this to yourself. You can play the coulda-shoulda game all day but it's not going to change anything. By finding where he's been doing this, we now have a little more info on him that we didn't have before. This could be the thing that helps us catch him."

"I want to catch him," she murmured, wiping at the tears streaming down her cheeks. "I want him to pay for what he did to her. How did he kill her? He'd done so much to her; please tell me he killed her quickly."

Tyler pulled away slightly, but wouldn't look her in the eye. Before she could ask another question, her hospital room door opened and three men walked in.

"I see you're awake, Ms. Alcott," the doctor said with a smile. "How are you feeling?"

"I've been better," she replied with a sniff, glancing past the man in green scrubs to the two men behind him.

One wore slacks and a tie, his older face set in a firm scowl, his gray military cut making him look all the more gruff and stern. Beside him stood a man who looked just like Tyler. Twins? He stood much taller than the older, military looking man, his wide shoulders encased in a blue denim shirt, his jeans hugging a trim waist and hips. The sleeves of his shirt were rolled up, showing off strong, tanned arms covered in black hair.

She glanced back and forth between the twins and realized the nameless twin's hair was much shorter. Tyler kept his longer, the ends curling enticingly around his collar. She wondered if they did that on purpose so people could tell them apart or if it had more to do with their own personal preferences.

"You haven't eaten in a couple of days, Ms. Alcott --" the doctor began.

"Please, Kaycee," she murmured, unable for the life of her to remember the doctor's name. She could remember his face, but that was about it.

The doctor nodded. "Kaycee."

"Why is there so much I can't remember?"

The doctor smiled slightly. "You've been pretty drugged up. That's part of the reason you haven't eaten. Most of the last couple of days will be a blur to you. Some of it you won't remember at all." The doctor tilted Kaycee's head, examining her sore eye. "It's looking better," he said with a slight grin as he moved to lift the sheet covering her feet. "I want you to try and eat something. Even if it's just soup. Okay? I also don't want you on these feet just yet. Give them another day, at least."

Kaycee nodded, still slightly confused and muddled. Her heart ached for Miranda and her inability to help her. Guilt ate at her stomach so much she wasn't sure she would be able to hold anything down.

"I'll see that she eats," Tyler said, then raised his eyebrow toward her with a firm look that spoke volumes. This man wouldn't take no for an answer.

Dropping her gaze from his, she pulled at the hospital gown with disgust. "Can someone call my assistant and tell her to bring me some more clothes?" she asked. "This gown is terribly uncomfortable."

"Uhmm," the other twin began as he stepped forward a couple of feet, a frown pulling at his brow. "You're no longer in New York, sweetheart. Don't you remember?"

She scowled at him. "What do you mean I'm no longer in New York? Where am I?"

Tyler put his hand on her thigh, and even through the blanket she could feel his heat seeping into her flesh. "You're in Knoxville, Tennessee, at the University of Tennessee Hospital. We found you in Blount County, close to the Smoky Mountains. They had to life flight you here."

She blinked; flashes of the helicopter and paramedics swarming around her ran through her mind. A policeman had come to the emergency room with her and, if she remembered correctly, never left her side.

"How did he get me *here*?" she asked softly.

"By car is my guess," the other twin replied, answering her question. "I'm Sam, by the way. Tyler's twin." He nodded toward Tyler, then waved a hand toward the man behind him. "And this is Agent Barreck. He's in charge of this case."

"Are you also a profiler?"

"Yes," Sam said, his lips lifting in a slight smile.

Her gaze flicked back and forth between the twins. Except for the hair, they were identical. The same beautiful blue eyes, the same deep tan and rugged good looks, the same hard and thick bodies. In their jeans, they looked like cowboys. All they needed were the hats.

"So, if he brought me here by car, how long was I out?"

"I would say at least twenty-four hours. Maybe more," Tyler answered.

"Oh my god." She sighed. "What's the date?"

"January twelfth," Sam replied.

"Twelfth?" she gasped. "You mean to tell me it's been four days since he took me?"

Tyler nodded. It felt like the photo shoot had been yesterday, not almost five days ago. With a sick feeling, her mind again turned to Miranda. "You never answered my question, Tyler. About Miranda."

Agent Barreck started to speak, but Tyler spoke up, interrupting him. "She died quickly."

Kaycee watched Barreck and Tyler exchange a look and she frowned, wondering what they could be hiding from her. The doctor patted her knee and flipped her chart closed before hanging it back at the foot of her bed. "I'll go see about getting you something to eat. Don't overdo it."

"Thank you," Kaycee said with a slight nod.

She doubted she'd be overdoing anything. Her strength had already begun to dwindle. With a frown, she remembered the pictures on the corkboard and what Miranda had said about looking like her.

"There were pictures of me everywhere. Do you think I know this guy?"

Tyler nodded. "It's possible, but you don't have to. Did you recognize anything about this guy? Anything about his voice seem familiar?"

Kaycee frowned, trying to remember. "His voice had been disguised, I think. It sounded weird -- almost like the voice a computer would use. If he kills them, then why does he keep his face covered? It's not like they could identify him."

Sam wiped at his lips. "Because he tapes it."

Kaycee's eyes widened. "He does what?"

Tyler shot Sam a scowl, before turning back to Kaycee. "He tapes it. We found his video equipment hidden behind a panel, but we didn't find the tapes. He apparently took those with him."

With a snort, Kaycee waved one hand. "So he can what? Make his own sick movie?"

"Yes. With you as the star."

With a gasp, she turned to stare at Agent Barreck.

"Barreck --" Tyler began, but Barreck held up his palm, quieting him.

"If we're going to keep her safe, she needs to know the whole truth, not just what you choose to tell her. It's obvious, Kaycee, that he's after you. Now what we need to do is figure out why."

"And, of course, who," she snapped snidely, making Sam's lips twitch in amusement. "I mean how can you figure out the why without first knowing the who?"

"Sometimes you can get to the why first. His murders are brutal, Kaycee. His victims mutilated, tortured," Sam offered.

"Sounds like he's angry," she murmured, shuddering as images of Miranda flashed through her mind.

"Yes. Possibly scorned."

She shook her head. "But I haven't scorned anyone. Hell, I haven't even been on a date in over two years. And I couldn't even tell you the last time I slept with someone."

Tyler snickered. "It doesn't have to be someone you've been out with. It could be someone who just thinks he's been scorned. Someone who hasn't even met you, but feels as though you've turned your back on him."

"Wow," she said sarcastically. She was getting tired, scared. "That certainly narrows it down, doesn't it?" She crossed her arms over her chest, hugging herself. "So what do you think he'll do now that I've gotten away? Will he try to get me again?"

"Definitely. That's why you're going with us," Tyler replied.

"Uhm, Tyler." Sam frowned, then pointed toward the door. "Can I talk to you out in the hall for a minute?"

Tyler followed Sam out into the hall, making sure the door was shut behind him. With a nod to the officer stationed outside, he led Sam a few feet away so they could talk in private. He had a pretty good idea what his brother would have to say.

"Are you out of your damn mind?" Sam snapped.

With a sigh, Tyler held up his hand, indicating Sam should keep his voice a little lower. "I'm not out of my mind, I just…"

"Just what? Think she's the one?" Sam growled. "I know you're attracted to her, Tyler, so don't even try to tell me this isn't about that. There're other FBI agents out there that can handle this one. Our ranch is not a safe house. It's not set up to be a safe house. It doesn't have the proper security."

"It's in the middle of fucking nowhere! You can't get any safer than that. And what's with you? Why do you think I can't bring this girl to the ranch and not fall for her?"

"Because you're already halfway there," Sam snarled, then pointed down the hall toward her hospital room. "You haven't left her bedside since we got here. Damn it, I knew you got too close to her. What did you see, Tyler, when you connected with her? What did you feel that makes you think she's the one?"

"I don't know." He sighed. "It was just a gut feeling. Like she belonged to me."

Sam snorted. "Not just you, pal. Did you forget that if you fall in love, then so do I?"

"How could I forget?" Tyler snarled.

"I'm tired of this, Tyler. I'm tired of watching them walk away."

"So you're going to go the rest of your life and never fall in love with another woman?"

"She's a model." Tyler rolled his eyes and sighed, making Sam's anger rise another notch. "She spends ninety-five percent of her life in the public eye. Even if we were able to find a woman who could accept us both, I doubt it's her. How would she explain having two husbands because you know it would come out? Man, you're living in a dream world if you think it's even remotely possible."

"I'm not giving up on finding our one, Sam," Tyler said in a soft, firm voice.

Sam shook his head. "Tell Kaycee to make a list of things she needs. I'll go to her house and pack her a few bags."

Sam stomped down the hall and Tyler watched him go with a heavy heart. Sam was scared. He'd taken the last rejection pretty hard.

But Tyler knew he wasn't wrong about this. He'd connected with Kaycee on a deeper level than Sam could. He'd been closer to her than anyone else. He could still feel her and he refused to believe it was his imagination.

Kaycee was meant to be theirs; he knew it.

* * *

Tyler sat next to Kaycee watching her sleep. With the back of his finger, he brushed her bangs aside, wincing at the dark bruise covering her cheek. He could still sense the lingering emotions he'd felt when he'd merged with her --

possessiveness, belonging. Like a foreshadowing of the future, those emotions had tightened his chest. Even now, they remained.

With a frown, he laid his hand over hers, careful not to wake her. The slightly chilled flesh of her fingers made his own skin tingle. Closing his eyes, he tried to recapture that connection, but without his brother he knew it was useless. Sam would have to be touching her as well.

Opening his eyes, he found his brother watching him from the other side of Kaycee's bed. Worry lines edged across his forehead, and darkened his eyes. Without a word, Sam sat and placed his hand over her arm next to Tyler's. They both closed their eyes.

Warmth spread through Tyler as images flashed before his mind's eye. Warm sand, blue skies, ocean waves, a gentle breeze. She was dreaming, but Tyler could sense confusion deep inside her -- indecision. In his mind he saw Sam standing close to her. Sam met his eyes over Kaycee's head as she turned to study at him as well. She smiled, but uncertainty sparkled in her eyes.

Whether she knew it or not, she was attracted to both of them. Even in her sleep, she couldn't decide which one she liked more.

Sam let go of her arm, breaking the connection. Opening his eyes, Tyler looked over at him. "She's attracted to both of us, Sam."

"That doesn't mean a damn thing," Sam growled, then stood, quickly leaving the room.

With a sigh, Tyler once again watched him go.

* * *

Kaycee stood outside Sam and Tyler's ranch house in the small town of Dumas, Texas, just outside Amarillo, and stared at the massive log structure in surprise. She'd expected a farmhouse or something, not this two-story monstrosity greeting her. It had a huge wraparound porch, going all the way around the house. Beside it sat a three-car garage made out of the same logs. Slightly behind that was a huge barn with a coral filled with horses. It was quite beautiful and, for some strange reason, felt like home.

Hugging her jacket tighter against her chest, she turned to study Tyler as he pulled her bags from the back of the black Expedition. She could see his shoulder muscles flex even beneath the fabric of his shirt. Sam looked just as handsome, his face partially covered by the brim of his Stetson. Her cheeks still blushed as she remembered his teasing remarks about her fancy panties, as he'd called them.

Sam had been the one to fly back to New York for her clothes and any other personal belongings she might need while Tyler and Agent Barreck had stayed with her at the hospital.

She'd gotten little sleep over the last three days. Nightmares plagued her when she slept, while a growing desire for the twins plagued her during the day. She shook her head, turning her back on the two gorgeous men still unloading the car. It had to be the damsel in distress thing. She saw them as her saviors, her knights in shining armor. And of course they were identical twins, so to be physically attracted to one made it only reasonable she would be attracted to the other as well.

At least that's what she kept telling herself, anyway. That sounded so much better than being a sex-deprived slut.

"Welcome to our ranch," Sam said as he strolled past her and up the concrete walk toward the house, a suitcase in each hand.

Her gaze wandered down his wide back past his trim waist and firm ass to those tree trunks he called legs. Tyler was just as big but for some reason slightly more approachable than his brother. Sam was great -- friendly, loved to tease, but he kept his distance, kept part of himself closed down.

Tyler came to stand next to her. She felt his presence long before she heard him speak. She could even smell his scent on the afternoon breeze. He smelled woodsy, musky. Amazingly, he smelled just like Sam.

"He's just a bundle of warmth, isn't he?" Kaycee replied, a slight quirk of amusement to her lips.

With a soft snicker, Tyler offered her his elbow. She still had a little trouble walking due to all the cuts on her feet and welcomed his support as she took slow steps toward the house.

"He's been hurt a few times, so he keeps his distance now. Especially around women."

"That's terrible," she said. "About him being hurt, I mean." What woman in her right mind wouldn't want him as a boyfriend?

She stopped and studied the three steps leading to the porch with a frown.

"Do you need me to carry you?" Tyler asked.

She was definitely tempted, but with a sigh shook her head. She needed to do this in order to heal. The more she did on her own, the faster she would be her old self again.

Holding tighter to Tyler's arm, she slowly made her way up the steps. Once at the top, she turned to smile at her escort. He returned her grin with one of his own and her stomach flipped.

"Watch out," Sam yelled from somewhere inside the house. "You've got incoming."

Tyler turned just in time to catch a massive ball of fur as he practically launched himself onto Tyler's chest. With a laugh, Tyler scratched behind the excited golden retriever's ears. "Hey, boy. How've you been?"

The dog barked, and Kaycee smiled, watching the two of them. "He's a beautiful dog," she said with a laugh.

Tyler pushed the dog back to his feet and gave him a quick pat. "Kaycee, this is Duke. Duke...Kaycee."

Kaycee leaned down, placing her fingers before the dog's nose. He sniffed, then barked once before nudging his head under her hand. With a laugh, she ruffled his hair playfully. "Hello, Duke."

Sam whistled from inside the house and the dog went running, answering his master's call.

"We also have a cat. Her name is Duchess. She's probably patrolling the barn. She pretty much comes and goes as she pleases."

"Duke and Duchess?" she asked with a chuckle of amusement.

Tyler shrugged. "Our housekeeper found a litter of kittens by the barn. She was the only one to survive. With a dog named Duke, seemed fitting to name her Duchess. We keep her around for the entertainment value."

"Entertainment value?"

"Yeah. Watch her and Duke for a couple of days and you'll see what I mean."

With a grin, Kaycee followed Tyler into the huge entry hall of the log house.

Sam stood back, watching Kaycee as she carefully made her way around the massive stone fireplace separating the living area and entry hall. Her gaze took in everything from the fire burning in the grate to the huge two-story windows overlooking the ranch.

He knew his brother was attracted to her because he was. He should have tried harder to talk Tyler out of this, but Barreck had insisted he wanted them in charge of her protection. They hadn't met a woman yet who could handle both of them. For one night maybe, but never for a lifetime. It wasn't going to happen and they both knew it. To bring her here was only going to invite trouble. They would fall in love with her, only for her to walk away in the end, unable to commit to a ménage relationship.

His gaze wandered aimlessly over her hourglass figure -- her firm, rounded breasts; long dark brown hair that curled slightly on the ends; full, totally kissable lips; and an adorable upturned nose. She turned so he could see her perfectly rounded hips and he almost groaned out loud. He felt his brother staring at him and he turned to shoot Tyler a glare. Yep, this was definitely one hell of a bad idea.

"I put her bags in the downstairs bedroom. It has its own bath and she won't have to climb the stairs."

With that, Sam turned to head down the hall toward the kitchen. Hell, a bar would be better, but they didn't dare leave her alone. Even as careful as they'd been, they couldn't be one hundred percent certain they weren't followed. They had to think and act as though her stalker was right outside their doors, despite what her close proximity did to his sanity, as well as his cock. He adjusted the coarse denim material over the ever increasing bulge behind his zipper.

This was going to be one hell of a long assignment.

Chapter Three

Kaycee strolled into the living room and sat on the corner of the leather sofa closest to the fire. The heat felt good and she wrapped her cold fingers around her coffee cup with a sigh. They'd given the housekeeper, Althea, a couple of weeks off, so Sam was handling the cooking, and doing a pretty good job of it, too. Although Althea had argued, they'd insisted they didn't want her there for her own safety. The less people they had around as targets, the better.

Her gaze strayed from the fire to Tyler, who sat in one of the oversized leather recliners across from her, his attention glued to the ledgers in his hand. The calico cat, Duchess, lay sprawled out on the back of the empty recliner next to him, her purrs of contentment filling the quiet room.

All through dinner, she'd felt an underlying tension between Tyler and Sam. She'd wanted to ask about it, but both of them kept distracting her with questions and heated stares when they thought she wasn't looking. Could it be they were attracted to her like she was to them?

"Here comes trouble," Tyler said softly.

She looked at him and he nodded to the dog, Duke. He stood a few feet from the empty recliner, his gaze narrowing on Duchess. She watched silently, wondering what the dog was up to when suddenly, he sprinted forward. His front paws landed on the seat, rocking the recliner forward with a jerk and sending an unsuspecting Duchess flying across the room to land on the couch next to Kaycee. Duchess rebounded quickly, hissing at the dog from her spot on the cushions.

Kaycee could have sworn Duke was laughing at the cat and put her hand over her mouth to stifle her own giggle. Tyler, on the other hand, sat in the recliner belly laughing -- his rich, deep baritone voice booming across the room, his whole body shaking as he threw his head back against the seat. Kaycee's amusement fled as the sound of his laughter heated her body.

"See what I mean about entertainment?" Tyler said with a grin and her stomach flipped.

"That's terrible," she chided as she reached out to stroke the cat's fur. "Poor Duchess."

"I promise, Duchess will retaliate," Sam replied as he stepped into the room and leaned his forearms against the back of the recliner, rocking it toward him. "And probably when Duke least expects it."

Kaycee's eyes dropped to the three open buttons at the top of his shirt where she could see the firm, tanned skin stretching tight across his muscles. Clearing her throat, she turned her attention back to the cat. "Do they do that kind of stuff all the time?"

"That's nothing," Tyler said with a chuckle. "It's a love-hate relationship with those two. We took Duchess to the vet once for a few days and Duke moped around like he'd lost his best friend." His gaze shot to Sam. "Kind of like Sam mopes when he doesn't get his way."

Sam snorted. "Kiss my ass."

Kaycee's lips twitched as she stared at Sam. "Do you mope, Sam?"

Rolling his eyes, Sam moved to drop into the recliner, his fingers absently rubbing at Duke's ears. In the back of her mind, she wondered what it would be like to have him stroke her neck and ears. "I do not mope, although I will admit to pouting a time or two in my younger days."

She grinned, trying to imagine Sam pouting. "I can't quite picture that. What does a pouting Sam look like?"

Tyler glanced back at the ledger, his lips twitching adorably. "Same as the moping Sam."

Sam shot Tyler a glare and Kaycee couldn't stop the giggle that slipped from her chest. These two were almost as entertaining as the animals. Sam's gaze locked with hers, and she could feel the heat clear across the few feet separating them. Her nipples hardened behind the cotton of her bra and she silently prayed he wouldn't notice. If he did, she would be incredibly embarrassed. She quickly changed the subject.

"So what is it exactly we're supposed to be doing?" Sam's eyebrow rose a fraction and she licked her lips, trying to ignore the tightening of her stomach. "Are we just hiding out while we wait for him to try something else?"

"For now," Sam replied, his stare dropping to her mouth. "You need time to heal."

Tyler threw a small pillow at Sam, catching him in the chest. Sam's eyes closed, then when he opened them back up, the heat was gone, replaced with a slight hint of irritation. What the hell was that all about? She turned her gaze to Tyler, but he didn't meet her stare, instead keeping it lowered on the ledgers.

With a sigh, Kaycee stood and handed her empty cup to Sam. "I think I'm going to turn in. That flight earlier today wore me out."

Sam nodded. "There's an extra blanket in the closet if you need it, and the remote for the TV is on the nightstand, in case you want to watch something."

"Thanks." She gave each of them a smile. "Good night."

"Good night, Kaycee," they replied in unison, and she resisted the urge to shudder at their deep, sexy voices.

"What the hell was the pillow for?" Sam snarled after Kaycee had left the room.

Tyler's gaze shot back to the closed bedroom door at the end of the short hallway, then back to his brother who stared daggers at him from the other chair.

"You were making her nervous, looking at her like you wanted to eat her alive. I doubt she's quite ready for that."

"I didn't even realize I was doing it." Sam sighed. "But you're probably right. A man staring at her in lust is most likely the last thing she wants to see right now."

Tyler snorted and slapped the ledger closed. "Do you have any idea how much time we would save if you would just keep 'Tyler's right' in your mind as a given?"

Sam shook his head in amusement. Throwing his head back, he stared at the ceiling. "Even though I pitched a fit, was completely against this whole thing, I keep thinking 'what if.'"

"I know."

Every woman they'd ever fallen for ended up leaving once she found out just what kind of relationship he and his brother wanted. Hell, needed. Tyler couldn't marry a woman and then expect Sam to never touch her. Sam would love her and want her just as much as he would. It would be hell for all of them.

"She's attracted to both of us," Tyler said.

"Yeah, I know. But we've had women attracted to both of us before. They were just never attracted to us equally."

Sam's gaze remained locked on the ceiling and Tyler detected a hint of sadness in his voice. His gaze narrowed and his head tilted slightly. Tyler frowned and looked up, trying to see what Sam did.

"What?" Tyler asked.

"I need to fix that skylight. Looks like it might be leaking."

"It's probably a shadow. Damn thing's not that old."

"Yeah, but you're the one who put it in." Sam looked over at him with a cheeky grin, making Tyler frown.

* * *

Two sets of warm, gentle hands skimmed along her thighs, making her tremble. Sandwiched between them, Kaycee felt safe, hot. Tyler nibbled along her neck, while Sam lifted the breast closest to him and drew his tongue around her nipple in teasing circles. She moaned, arching her back to thrust her breast more fully into his mouth, but he backed away, continuing to tease her relentlessly.

Tyler's hand skimmed lower, then slowly back up the inside of her thigh with featherlight touches. As he came close to her aching pussy, her hips rose, seeking his touch. But instead, he brushed the back of his fingers along the skin just above her clit. She shuddered, desperate for more.

Sam's kisses moved lower, along her trembling stomach as Tyler moved to nip at the underside of her breast. She gasped, letting her legs fall wide, allowing Sam access to her sopping entrance. Every part of her burned with need. She could hardly breathe from the lust coursing through her veins.

Tyler put a hand behind her thigh and lifted it, holding it high so Sam could settle himself easily between her splayed legs. His hot breathe hit her slit and she gasped, lifting her hips higher. With one palm at the back of her other thigh, he pressed it back, spreading her even wider.

Two thick fingers entered her, making her moan in pleasure. "So wet, baby," Sam purred, then removed his fingers to slide them along her pulsing slit, separating her labia.

She whimpered, tossing her head from side to side as both men continued to fondle her, torment her. Tyler's teeth scraped at her engorged nipple, making her gasp as Sam drew his tongue along her slit in a sensual draw that had her grinding her pussy against his face.

"You taste good, Kaycee," Sam whispered as he licked his tongue inside her channel, making her cream against his lips.

The pressure inside her built as Sam continued to lick his fill. Tyler's lips moved to her ear as his fingers played and tugged at her nipples. "Does it feel good, baby?" he whispered. "Do you like having Sam eat your pussy?"

"Yes," she whimpered, lifting her hips off the mattress as Sam drew slow circles around her clit with the tip of his tongue.

Tyler removed his hand from her breast and slid one thick finger into her mouth. She sucked at it hungrily and he groaned. "I want to feel you do that to my cock. I want to feel those sweet lips wrap around my cock while Sam fucks your pussy."

She was on fire now. Hot, burning, intensifying fire.

Tyler removed his finger and dropped his mouth back to her breasts, this time engulfing the entire tip with his hot mouth. She groaned, arching her back. Her whole body wiggled and squirmed, desperate for that explosive pleasure that kept building inside her.

They took her higher until she thought she'd burst. Sam flattened his tongue against her clit and she screamed, every part of her tingling with intense pleasure as her orgasm raced through her. Sam continued to lick and torment, wringing even more out of her as she floated back down.

"So beautiful," Tyler whispered.

Kaycee opened her eyes with a start, her body still humming from the release she'd experienced in her dream. Her skin was covered in sweat, her fingers gripping the sheet beneath her, her breathing still erratic and harsh.

"Oh my, God," she gasped, swallowing hard as remnants of the dream flashed through her mind.

Is that what it's like to be with two men?

Wow.

Slowly, she released her death grip on the sheets and sat up, brushing her hair from her face with trembling fingers. "This is nuts," she murmured to herself. "I can't keep having dreams like that. I'll embarrass the hell out of myself."

Her gaze moved to the ceiling and she cringed, closing her eyes tight. "Oh, God. I hope I didn't get that loud for real."

Talk about embarrassment.

Her stomach growled and she glanced at the clock. Two in the morning. Surely Sam and Tyler were already in bed. It should be safe to sneak into the kitchen for a late-night snack. Or early morning snack, depending on how one looked at it.

She slung her legs over the side of the bed and reached to the floor for her slippers before heading to the kitchen. The lights were off, but there was more than enough moonlight shining through the window to guide her way. White streaks of light slashed across the floor in diagonal patterns, creating an intriguing design. Paying more attention to the floor than where she was going, she raised her eyes and immediately noticed a dark form at the oversized kitchen island.

She jumped, letting out a squeal before realizing it was Tyler. "You scared me," she breathed, putting her hand over her pounding heart.

"I'm sorry. You okay?"

She nodded, taking a deep breath for control. "Yeah. Why are you in the dark?"

He shrugged and switched on the light over the sink, casting a soft yellow glow over the granite counter tops. "I very seldom turn on the lights. I know the house well enough I don't have to."

"Of course," she said with a nod. She did the same thing at home.

Tyler held up a sandwich. "Hungry?"

"Starving," she admitted, reluctantly.

After her dream, she almost wished he'd left the lights out so he couldn't see the blush rising quickly up her cheeks. She couldn't stop stealing glances at his bare chest. Smooth, tanned skin pulled taut over hard muscles, and a six-pack she could crack an egg on practically had her salivating. There were models out there that didn't look that good. Add to that the flannel pajama pants hanging low on his lean hips and she might as well accept the fact she was a goner.

"Ham or turkey?"

She frowned at Tyler's question, then shook her head, forcing herself to concentrate on something other than his physique. "Uh, ham."

He went back to fixing the sandwich, his eyes lowered. "Trouble sleeping?"

She nodded and sat on one of the island stools across from him.

"A little. Bad dreams," she added as an afterthought, but kept her eyes on the countertop instead of his intense scrutiny.

"Considering the circumstances, it's understandable."

"Mmmm," she murmured, thinking not of her attacker, but of how Tyler's fingers had plucked at her nipples. Glancing down, she noticed with mortification that her nipples had begun to harden and poke through her tank top.

God, this is nuts.

She crossed her arms in the hopes of hiding the evidence of her surprising arousal. Tyler said something and she looked across the island at him with a frown. His deep blue eyes twinkled with amusement, mesmerizing her. "I'm sorry. What?" she asked.

One corner of his mouth twitched, making his eyes sparkle. "I said you're not what I expected. Being a model and all."

She scowled. She hated it when people made snap judgments about her just because she modeled. "Meaning?"

"I get the feeling that came out wrong," he said with a grin. He put the sandwich on a napkin and passed it across the counter. "I didn't mean for it to. To be honest, I almost expected you to barely eat enough to stay alive and lay in the bed making demands like a queen."

"Not all models are like that," she grumbled.

He nodded, his lips morphing into an amazingly sexy smile that made her insides tingle. "I stand corrected."

"Do you and Sam live here in this big house alone?" she asked, trying to change the subject and maybe find out a little more about them.

Watching him closely, she took a bite of her sandwich.

"Yes. We had it built two years ago."

"What if one of you gets married?"

Tyler shrugged. "We probably won't."

She frowned. "Why? Not into women?"

He snorted, then glanced toward the bay window on the other side of the breakfast nook.

"We're definitely into women, but women...well, let's just say there aren't too many women out there that could handle mine and Sam's sexual demands."

She stopped chewing and stared at him in trepidation. "Just what kind of sexual demands do you have?" she asked, then quickly wiped at her chin to remove the bread that had flown out during her surprised outburst. Her cheeks heating, she hoped she hadn't looked too ridiculous.

Tyler pursed his lips and breathed a long sigh through his nose. His gaze narrowed slightly in indecision before meeting hers head on.

"Sam and I are unusual twins. We're identical; that's obvious and partly why I keep my hair longer than his."

"So people can tell you apart," she offered.

"Yes. It makes it easier dealing with people who don't know us well enough to tell us apart through the way we speak or through our personalities."

Kaycee nodded and took another bite of her sandwich. With a wave of her hand, she encouraged him to continue.

"We found out early on that Sam and I are also connected mentally. My mother used to always say we were two halves of the same soul split into separate bodies. When Sam gets hurt, I feel it. When he loves, I feel it also."

Kaycee set her remaining sandwich on the napkin, intrigued. "So if Sam falls in love with a woman, you would fall in love with her too?"

Tyler nodded. "Yes. And vice versa."

She frowned. "So what does that have to do with the sexual...oh," she said, as it finally hit her. "You would want to share her."

Tyler nodded, his lips twitching slightly as amusement lit up his eyes, making them darker.

"So you haven't been able to find a woman who would agree to that."

"We've shared before. Many times. But women don't want that *all the time*. It was a fun fantasy to be fulfilled, but the realization of having to satisfy two men with very healthy sexual appetites, I guess, was a bit daunting to them."

"So they ran," she said.

Tyler nodded. "As fast as they could."

"Well, I have to admit, having to satisfy one man can be a bit overwhelming sometimes. I couldn't imagine having to take care of two."

Tyler leaned his hips against the counter behind him, his arms crossing over his wide chest. He stared down at her, his eyes sparkling with merriment. "So you think satisfying a man in bed is overwhelming?"

"Well, sometimes, yeah. There's day-to-day life that gets in the way. You're tired or don't feel well or work was crappy. It's hard enough to have to satisfy one man and you're asking women to take care of two?"

Tyler shrugged. "We are what we are. How would it work if Sam married a woman and I always had to stay on the sidelines, loving her from a distance? As long as Sam loved her, I would love her. And if I did decide to try and make it work with someone else, how fair would that be to them? I would still be in love with Sam's wife. I would still desire her. Want her just like Sam would. That would make for one lousy relationship for all involved."

"Well, I suppose you have a point there," she relented.

"How about we get back to this 'satisfying men is overwhelming to you.'"

"Overwhelming was probably the wrong word to use, okay? It's not overwhelming; it's just…not worth it sometimes. Most of the men I've been with didn't have a clue how to satisfy a woman."

That was an understatement. Half the guys she'd had the displeasure of being with didn't have a clue, and the other half…well, they were even worse.

Tyler laughed. Kaycee frowned. She hated it when men laughed like that. So condescendingly. Kaycee snorted. Like he was any different than all the others. "You think that's funny? You think you're any better at finding a woman's clit or G-spot?"

Heat instantly flared across her cheeks as she stared at his still chuckling form leaning nonchalantly against the counter, his eyebrow raised adorably. She spoke before thinking *way* too much.

"Maybe," he drawled in that deep, sexy voice of his, and liquid heat pooled in her belly.

What the hell had she been thinking to say something like that? And what was with her and these instant, lustful reactions? She'd been around gorgeous men before. What was it about these two that set her blood on fire?

"How did we even get on this subject, anyway?" she grumbled. "I think I should probably go back to bed."

Turning, she headed back through the living room. Her gaze fell on the pillow and blanket thrown across the leather sofa and she stopped. "Tyler," she yelled.

"Yeah?" he asked softly from behind her and she jumped, not expecting him to be that close.

Turning, she found herself almost nose-to-chest with his hard body, then quickly stepped back. "You're sleeping in here?"

He nodded. "Sam and I are taking turns sleeping on the sofa. That way we're close if anything were to happen."

"Oh," she said.

With a nervous nod, she began to walk backward toward her room.

"Did you know you talk in your sleep?" he asked, his voice dropping sensually.

She stopped and stared at him, her breathing quick and shallow. What had he heard? Or more importantly, what had she said?

"That's what woke me," he added, his lips quirking slightly, his piercing gaze full of heat and threatening to burn her very flesh.

Oh, God. He knew. He knew what she'd been dreaming about, she'd bet her last dollar. Lifting her chin, she glared, hoping to disguise her blush of embarrassment as anger.

"If you were a gentleman, you would have kept that little bit of information to yourself."

"And miss that tell-tale blush? Hell, no," he drawled, his lips spreading into a knowing grin.

She spun on her heel, heading quickly to the bedroom. Once inside, she slammed the door shut.

Damn arrogant cowboy.

Chapter Four

Closing the gate behind her with a click, Kaycee followed Tyler into the barn. The weather was fairly warm for January, the sunshine bright and the sky a beautiful blue, just about two shades lighter than Tyler's eyes. It was turning out to be a gorgeous day and she was actually excited about working with the horses. So much so that she could almost forget about her dream from the night before.

Well, almost, that is.

Her gaze strayed to Tyler's jean-covered ass. Levi's never looked so damn good. Sam was just as handsome, even if he did spend the entire morning walking around with a scowl on his face.

Over the last few days she'd noticed a difference in the two of them. Sam gave off a strong alpha male vibe while Tyler had a quieter, more fun-loving nature. Or maybe it just seemed that way because Sam was so pissed about something right now that his fun-loving side didn't show through. Tyler was definitely easier to talk to, but that was probably because she'd spent more time with him.

"What can I do to help?" she asked, stuffing her hands in her jean pockets.

Tyler glanced at her over his shoulder. "Can you ride?"

She shrugged. *Can I ride?* She'd grown up on horses, but he didn't have to know that just yet. "Yeah, I think so."

"Okay. You can ride around the pastures with me. Make sure we don't have any fences down, that sort of thing."

Kaycee nodded, her teeth nibbling on her lower lip. She'd been trying all morning to not think about her attacker. She felt safe with Tyler and Sam. More so than she'd felt since the whole incident had happened. And she felt at home on their ranch -- like she belonged. But that was crazy, wasn't it?

Sighing, she turned to study the twelve stalls -- six down each side of the barn and each filled with a beautiful horse. Coming to the first stall on the right, she reached her hand out to stroke the nose of a solid black mare.

"What's your name?" she whispered.

"Midnight," Tyler said from behind her, making his voice whinny like a horse and she threw him a smile over her shoulder.

"Real cute," she said with a chuckle.

"She's a little wild," he said with a nod toward the horse. "Think you can handle that one?"

Turning back to the horse, she stroked her palm down her neck. "I think we'll be just fine. Won't we, Midnight?"

The horse nodded, blowing air out her nostrils, making Kaycee giggle.

"All right," Tyler drawled. "But don't say I didn't warn ya."

Kaycee took the bridle he held out to her and opened the stall door to slip it over the horse's neck.

"Bring her down to the other end while I get the saddles from the tack room."

Kaycee led the horse to the far end, talking to her all the while. Her parents had made her take riding lessons when she was younger. By the time she was fourteen, she'd won numerous trophies and ribbons. She looked forward to getting back on a horse and enjoying the freedom of the wind whipping through her hair as she and Midnight sped across the fields, working across the land as one.

Standing back, she watched in admiration as Tyler threw the saddle over the back of the horse. His sleeves were rolled up past his forearms, showing off rippling muscles while hers twitched in response. She should know better than to fall for the FBI agents assigned to protect her. It would be nuts, especially after what Tyler had told her last night. If she loved one, they would expect her to love the other as well.

An intriguing thought, but how would it be realistically?

After cinching the saddle tight, Tyler patted Midnight's haunches. "You're all set." His gaze met hers over the saddle. "Stay close to me."

"I will."

He nodded then went to climb on his own horse -- a chestnut Arabian named Charlie. Kaycee put her foot in the stirrups, lifting herself up to throw her free leg over the saddle and smiled at the unusual names they came up with for their animals. Midnight shifted at the added weight and pranced . Kaycee could feel the coiled tension in the horse beneath her -- the desire to run.

Kaycee felt that desire too -- the need to be carefree, to leave her worries and fears behind. Leaning down, she whispered softly in the horse's ear, "Run, Midnight."

With a kick of Kaycee's heels, the horse took off at breakneck speed out of the barn. Kaycee laughed and turned her face to the wind, giving the horse free rein to run where she wanted.

She thought Tyler would follow. She thought he would enjoy the run as much as she was, but the second she heard his voice booming angrily behind her, she knew she'd been wrong. Pulling at the reins, she brought Midnight to stop just as a furious Tyler circled around the front of her horse, then came to a stop next to her, facing the opposite direction.

He reached out his hands, grabbing her wrists and dragging her from the saddle. Midnight pranced away and Kaycee squealed as Tyler hauled her ass over the horn of own his saddle. With a gasp, she struggled to regain her balance and maneuvered her leg over the side of the horse, causing her to straddle Tyler's thighs, facing him.

She gasped in shock, unsure how it had all happened so quickly.

"Damn it, woman," Tyler growled, anger flaring in his eyes. She bent backward, trying to put some space between her and a gorgeously furious Tyler. "You can't run off like that." He gave her wrists a rough shake. "You can't ever forget he's still out there. He could be right there." His finger pointed to a hill not far away. "He could be watching us, watching you."

Glancing toward the hill, she swallowed a lump of fear, almost half afraid she'd see someone. But no one stood there.

No one watched. She turned back to Tyler who still glared at her with barely controlled anger, and the reality of her position hit her in the face like a splash of cold water. She wasn't even sure how she'd gotten like this.

Her thighs straddled Tyler's, her pussy lying directly against his cock. Her gaze was level with his angry stare that now began to register a little of the surprise she felt. His fingers still clenched her wrists and he pulled back slightly, tugging her the last few inches that separated them so that her breasts flattened against his chest. She gasped softly, and felt her eyes widen as she gazed into his, their noses touching.

"How the hell did we manage this?" he whispered, and his breath brushed across her lips, making her shudder.

Tyler must have felt it. Even this close, she could see his eyes close, then open and pierce her with their heat. She swallowed and backed away, putting some much-needed space between them again, but the second she felt the loss of his body against hers, she regretted it. "I think I did it to keep from falling when you pulled me over."

She couldn't stop staring at him, couldn't stop inhaling his musky scent mingled with hay, horseflesh, and the outdoors. His gaze dropped to her mouth and her heart jumped in her chest. In reflex, she licked her lips and Tyler watched every single flick of her tongue as it glided across her bottom lip.

He let her hands drop to her thighs but kept his fingers wrapped around her wrists. She could hardly breathe. She'd never wanted someone to kiss her so much in her life. He'd been so considerate to her the last few days. So kind. Gentle.

Well, the tug from the horse hadn't been gentle, but that didn't count. After all, he was right. She shouldn't have done it. And God help her, she had this same intense reaction to Sam.

She could feel the heat radiating off Tyler in waves. The sexual tension hung between them like something tangible, touchable. Would a ménage relationship with the two of them really be that hard? Or would it be easy? Easy because it felt right? But she'd never been with two men -- never even contemplated it.

"Damn, Kaycee," he murmured, and his mouth moved just a hair closer, his breath hot as it fanned across her lips.

Tyler's lips brushed across hers with the barest of touches and her mouth parted, inviting the invasion of his tongue. With a sigh, she tried hard to keep from grinding her pussy against his thick bulge. God, it felt good and so damn big.

"Do you have any idea what you're inviting?" he breathed across her mouth as he dropped the reins and moved her wrists to the small of her back, holding them together and immobile. Her heart pounded in fear for a fleeting second, then passion returned. Tyler would never hurt her. She knew it.

"If you get me, you get Sam, too," he whispered, then licked his tongue across her bottom lip, making her shudder.

"Would you be okay with that, Kay?" he asked as one hand moved over her jean-clad hip, sending tingles along her limbs. "Would you let both of us take you at once?"

Her stomach knotted as images ran through her mind. Images of her sandwiched between them. She gasped softly at his words, shocked that what he was saying would turn her on like this. Her panties were soaked as her juices continued to pour from her pussy. Her nipples hardened painfully, aching for his mouth. Hell, right now even his hand would do.

His palm gripped her hip, shifting her pussy over his cock and she closed her eyes on a groan as sharp, piercing tingles of pleasure raced up her back and tightened her womb.

"Tyler," she sighed just before his lips covered hers in a kiss that stole the very breath from her lungs.

He let go of her wrists and better positioned her over his cock. She moaned, wrapping her arms around his neck and sliding her fingers through his soft hair. His mouth devoured hers; his tongue wreaked havoc on her mind as well as her body.

"You're so damn pretty," he murmured against her lips.

The horse shifted beneath them, causing her mound to shift against his hard shaft. They both groaned, the kiss deepening as he ate at her mouth hungrily. His palms moved her hips, grinding her against him in a rhythm that nearly sent her over the edge. She was so close. The extra friction the clothing provided against her clit as they moved against each other felt like heaven.

His lips broke away from hers to blaze a hot trail down the side of her neck. She felt weak, dizzy as his teeth scraped across the sensitive flesh behind her ear. His palm moved upward to cup her breast, squeezing it through the material of her shirt and jacket. She wanted their clothes off, to feel the heat of his skin beneath her touch, to feel his cock stretching her until she begged him to stop.

Tyler knew he was doing something he shouldn't. Sam would know the second he saw him what he'd done. What he wanted so badly to do. But he hadn't been able to stop himself. From the second he realized where her pussy was sitting, he'd been fighting a losing battle. Hell, he'd been fighting this damn losing battle from the second he'd laid eyes on her -- from the second he'd connected with her -- felt her strength, her courage.

He knew deep in his gut she was the one for him and Sam. He knew it the second her lips touched his. It felt more right than it ever had with any other woman. But would she run like all the others -- afraid she wouldn't be able to handle it, to handle both him and his brother? Because God knew they could be demanding. Both of them were dominant, aggressive. Both of them would want her to submit -- to be theirs forever. Both of them would require things of her she might not be ready for. Especially after what had happened to her.

But God, she felt good. The way her pussy rubbed against his shaft, her heat seeping through their pants straight to his balls; even her mewling whimpers and breathy moans drove him wild.

He'd bet she tasted like heaven. Like pure honey.

Her body shuddered in his arms. She was so close. He could feel it in the way her upper body tensed, in the way her hips moved faster. With a loud cry, she threw her head back, grinding her hips in a circular motion against his cock.

He ground his teeth to keep from throwing her from the horse and ripping her clothes off, burying his aching rod into the soft heat of her pussy, so damn deep she would scream.

She pressed down harder and he groaned into her neck. "That's it, baby," he coaxed. "Come for me."

Every part of her trembled in his embrace as she rode out her orgasm, rotating her hips against him. He pressed upward, intensifying her pleasure, giving her more. He wanted to be inside her so much he hurt -- ached so bad his balls felt as though they would burst. Her body against his was so right, so perfect, and the intensity of it took his breath. With a sigh, she collapsed onto his chest and he held her tight, brushing his fingers through her hair.

"You let Midnight get away."

Kaycee tensed at the angry tone in Sam's voice. But Tyler didn't. He knew it wasn't Kaycee Sam was mad at. It was him.

"Oh, my God. Sam," she whispered into his neck.

Tyler looked over her head to see Sam a few feet away, the horse beneath him prancing in agitation, Midnight's reins in his hand.

"You both shouldn't be on Charlie, Tyler. He's too old for that shit."

Tyler nodded and scowled at Sam. His brother returned his scowl, silently letting him know this wasn't over. Dropping Midnight's reins, Sam turned his own horse and galloped away.

Kaycee sat up, her eyes full of unshed tears. "Sam," she called, but Tyler shook his head.

"Not now, Kaycee. Trust me."

"If not now" -- her troubled stare met his -- "then when?"

* * *

Kaycee strolled into the kitchen and pulled a Diet Coke from the fridge. Her stomach was in knots; her head ached, as did her heart. God, she felt like she'd cheated on Sam. How and why had she let things get that far?

It felt good, that's why. Right.

Letting out a heavy sigh, she dropped into one of the chairs surrounding the kitchen table. She still hadn't seen Sam, and even if she did she wasn't sure what she would say to him. She wasn't real sure what to say to Tyler either.

The ride back had been silent, tense. She didn't regret what she'd done, not really. If anything, she wanted more. But how much more she just didn't know. Could she handle both of them?

Tyler's boots stomped across the floor and she glanced up at his pensive frown as he entered the kitchen.

"Sam's refusing to cook dinner so it looks like it's just me and you." His gaze met her troubled look and his lips lifted into a half smile. "It's me he's mad at, Kaycee. Not you."

"Why is he mad at you?"

"Because I promised him I wouldn't do that. He thinks you'll run just like all the others have. He's scared."

"What? And I'm not? Hell, I don't even know what happened out there."

"Lust is what happened out there," Tyler said with a shrug.

He turned his back to her, heading to the fridge on the other side of the room, but she caught a glimpse of his eyes. He didn't believe that any more than she did. Yes, it had been lust -- but it had also been much more than that.

With an aggravated huff, she pushed her chair back and stood, leaving her Coke untouched on the table. "I'm going to talk to Sam."

"What are you going to tell him, Kaycee?" Tyler asked quietly, making her stop in her tracks.

She glanced at Tyler over her shoulder, confusion creasing her brow. "I don't know yet."

* * *

Sam threw the pitchfork across the stall in irritation. He'd known the second he'd seen Tyler's reaction to Kaycee that they were in trouble. He'd tried to tell him then to walk away, to not accept Barreck's assignment of keeping her hidden. She was a fucking model, for crying out loud. Always in the public eye, used to the fancy things in life. He and Tyler certainly weren't poor but there was no way she would agree to a life as wife to two men.

But he'd felt it too. The pull to be near her. The need to keep her close, to touch her, kiss her...possess her.

With a sigh, he leaned his palms against the wall, his head hanging low, his eyes closed. He could still see her face when she'd come in Tyler's arms. The flush of her cheeks, the grinding of her hips, the way she whimpered, then screamed. His cock became rock hard just from the memory. But worse than that, he felt Tyler's reaction -- felt both of them falling helplessly under her spell.

Their mother had told them once years ago she believed there was one woman out there made just for them -- one woman who would bring them together, forming a perfect family of three. Tyler believed Kaycee was that woman. Sam wasn't sure he could take another rejection if it turned out his brother was wrong.

"Sam."

He jerked in surprise stared straight into Kaycee's green eyes. She stood just a few feet away, wringing her hands like a nervous child, her stance screaming hesitancy, her brow drawn tight in concern.

"You shouldn't have walked out here alone, Kaycee. We have to act --"

"As though he's right outside the door, I know," she said with a nod. "But I wanted to talk to you."

He stepped away from the wall and grabbed the pitchfork he'd thrown just seconds before. "There's nothing to talk about."

"I feel terrible..."

His head snapped up. "Why? You have nothing to feel terrible about, Kaycee. This is between me and Tyler. It doesn't have anything --"

"Tyler told me," she interrupted.

He stared at her in shock, his fingers tightening on the wooden handle. "Tyler told you what?"

"About you and him. About how you feel the same things."

"Shit," Sam growled and dug his fingers through his hair. "That's..."

"That's what? Personal? None of my business?"

"Yes!" he snapped.

Her eyes narrowed in anger as they glared at one another, neither willing to back down. How had it come to this so fast? "It's only been a week, Kaycee. A fucking week and already I want you so bad I hurt. But not just physically. I want all of you. Does that make any sense to you at all? Because it doesn't to me. And Tyler!" he snapped pointing toward the house. "He feels the same way. How does that make you feel, knowing that both of us want to screw the hell out of you? Knowing that both of us want to dominate you, make you submit, fill you up with toys before we take you ourselves! Take you so deep you'll think we're coming out your throat!"

"Stop it! Why are you being such an ass?" she snapped back. "You don't think it's weird for me? I was just brutally attacked two weeks ago and yet here I am, perfectly ready and willing for the two of you to do just that! I don't understand it any more than you do! Stop trying to push me away! Stop trying to scare me into running because that's what you think I'm going to do anyway!"

"I'm not trying to scare you, Kaycee. I'm being honest."

She tilted up her chin, daring him, challenging him. And damned if he didn't love it. "And so am I. Maybe if you'd quit running scared, you'd see I'm still standing here."

"You don't have any choice in the matter, darlin'," he snarled. "Remember?"

"I'm tougher than I look, Sam."

"This doesn't have anything at all to do with being tough. It has to do with what you can accept. If you get into a relationship with Tyler, you get into one with me. That's how it is in this family." He took a step closer, his gaze dropping to the rise and fall of her chest. "And that relationship will include sex with us, individually and together. Can you handle *that*, Kaycee?"

His eyes moved back to her face and to her credit, she hadn't budged. She stood her ground, her chin raised, her shoulders set in determination.

"Can you handle it if I said yes?" she countered.

His lips twitched at her spunk. "I'll give you a day to think about it. Why don't you run back to the house and have sex with Tyler. That will give you an idea of what you're in for."

Her eyes narrowed. "Screw you, Sam."

With that, she turned on her heel and left the barn. He stood in the open doorway, keeping a close eye on her progress, along with the gentle swaying of her ass in those tight jeans. With a sigh, he swiped his hand down his mouth and chin. What the hell were they going to do with her?

He knew what he wanted to do with her. His brow cocked as ideas ran through his mind at alarming speed. Oh, yeah. He definitely knew what he wanted to do with her. Sure she was tough. She'd held her own against a serial killer and gotten away. She'd survived, pulled herself up by the bootstraps, and accepted them as her protectors, her guardians. But that didn't mean she would accept them as her lovers, and the thought of her rejection ate a hole straight through his chest.

If he felt this way after only a week, God help him if they had to stay together much longer.

* * *

Kaycee stomped through the entrance hall, her anger rising by the second. Sam, the one she thought was the easygoing one, the teasing one, had turned out to be the jerk. God, why did he have to be such an ass?

As she rounded the fireplace, she caught Tyler's concerned expression. He looked way too much like his brother for her to not be angry at him, too. "You're brother is a damn ass," she snapped, then stormed past him to the bedroom, slamming the door behind her.

Leaning her back against it, she closed her eyes tight, trying to stop the tears threatening to spill over. She didn't know what the hell to do or even what she wanted.

Tyler quirked a brow, then turned to glare at Sam as he, too, came through the front door. "What the hell did you say to her?"

"You don't want to know," Sam said as he dropped into the recliner. "Trust me."

"No. I think I do want to know."

"Let's just say I wasn't the nicest person to her."

"Damn it, Sam," Tyler growled, dragging his fingers through his hair as he paced to the fireplace. "What the hell is the matter with you?"

Sam narrowed his eyes. "What do you think? I hope that little semi-fuck session this afternoon was worth it. You're falling in love with her, I can feel it. And you know damn good and well, when you do, I do. I don't want to go through this again, Tyler. I don't want to have to stand back and watch yet another woman walk out of our lives because she can't handle it."

Tyler rounded on him in anger. "What makes you think she'll walk away?"

"What makes you think she won't?"

With a tired sigh, he shook his head. "I'm not backing down, Sam. I'm sorry, but I'm not giving up on her."

"It's only been a week. You take longer picking out a suit and you expect me to believe it's love? That you know for a fact, she's the one?"

"You feel what I feel, Sam. You tell me." Turning, he headed up the stairs to the second floor. "You get the couch tonight. Oh..." He slapped his hand against the wooden banister and stopped to stare at his brother over the railing. "When she starts screaming out our names in her sleep as she orgasms...she'll want something to eat afterward."

"What?" Sam gaped, but Tyler ignored him, heading upstairs. Let Sam find out for himself.

Chapter Five

Sam lay on the couch, his gaze glued to the rafters above. Damn Tyler. Duke walked over and laid his head on his thigh. Sam absently rubbed at his neck, his mind on Kaycee.

Tyler wasn't one to fall in love quickly, so that's what made this all so strange. But then Tyler was the one connecting with their targets on a more mental level. Sam could only see through their eyes. Tyler felt them, became them. Maybe that's what all this was with Kaycee. But that didn't explain Sam's own feelings.

It felt right -- her being here in this house. He and Tyler had built it with a huge master suite in anticipation of one day finding a wife to share. Unfortunately, a wife hadn't worked out. What would it be like to have Kaycee as a wife?

Damn, she was pretty. Sexy. And that ass. Just thinking about grabbing a handful made his cock spring to life.

But he couldn't stop thinking about the hurt he'd felt the one time he and Tyler had tried to make a relationship work. Jenny had been young, sweet, and maybe that had been the problem. She'd been too young, too inexperienced. He'd loved her so much and so had Tyler, but she'd run scared. She hadn't been able to let him and Tyler share her even once and had accused them of just using their connection as an excuse to have a ménage.

They couldn't make her understand. They couldn't make her see Tyler loved her as much as he did. In the end, it wasn't meant to be. Could he go through that again?

Duke's ears perked up and the dog raised his head, his gaze narrowing on Kaycee's door. He'd heard something and Sam perked up as well. "What did you hear, boy?" he asked, cocking his head to listen.

A moan. Soft, but it was definitely coming from Kaycee's room. Had Tyler been serious about her having sex dreams? Ah, hell. Sam sat up, listening closer as another one, louder this time came through. He tensed. That wasn't a sexy moan. She was scared.

Jumping up from the couch, he ran down the short hall and threw her door open, his heart pounding in anxiety. He immediately saw her on the bed, the covers kicked from her body, her face contorted into a frown, a light sheen of sweat dotting her brow.

"No," she whimpered, tossing her head.

She was in the middle of a nightmare. Rushing forward, he sat on the edge of the mattress and grabbed her shoulders, shaking them slightly. "Kaycee, wake up."

She gasped, her eyes opening wide and staring up at him in fear, then confusion.

"It's okay." He leaned over slightly, putting his palm flat on the mattress beside her shoulder. "You're safe. It was just a dream. You okay?"

She nodded, then shook her head, her lower lip trembling adorably. Fear still clouded her eyes and his gut clenched. It was the first sign of weakness or vulnerability he'd seen in her.

"I'm not," she whispered. Sitting up, she wrapped her arms around Sam's neck, holding tight as she sobbed into his chest.

At first he froze, surprised at her clinging, and the way her body seemed to fit so perfectly against his. With a sigh, he wrapped his arms around her back and held her close, letting her release her pent-up anxiety and fear.

"It's okay," he whispered.

His hand moved into her hair, enjoying the feel of her silky tresses as they wrapped around his fingers. He inhaled, catching the scent of sunshine and vanilla, and his whole body warmed. She smelled so good.

"I can still feel his hands on me," she whispered through her sobs.

He held her tighter, desperate to make her feel safe, secure. He wanted to protect her, comfort her. God, he wanted to kiss her. He rolled his eyes toward the ceiling. He was screwed, falling so deeply under her spell he could hardly breathe.

"It's just my hands on you, sweetheart," he murmured into her ear. "No one else's."

She nodded and her cheek rubbed against his bare chest, her warm tears wetting his skin.

"Come on. Lay down."

He eased her back onto the mattress, then moved over her thighs to lie on the bed next to her. She curled into him, fitting just right against his side. Raising an arm, he wrapped it around her waist and held her, his palm stroking slowly up and down her back.

"Want to talk about it?" he asked, trying to think of anything other than the feel of her breasts against his chest through the thin cotton of her tank top.

She shook her head.

"Might make you feel better."

Again she shook her head and he grinned slightly. "I'm sorry about earlier, Kaycee," he whispered. Maybe if they talked about what an ass he was, she would forget about the nightmare.

"So am I. I'm sorry I called you an ass to Tyler."

Her voice was muffled and he pulled back slightly so he could see her face. Her cheeks were still wet with tears and he wiped at them with his thumb. One corner of his lips lifted.

"You didn't tell him anything he didn't already know."

She smiled slightly. "Yeah. I kind of got that impression."

Sam chuckled. "Better now?"

"Yeah. Thanks," she said, then rolled to her back, her frown focused on the ceiling. "I get this feeling sometimes that there's something I'm missing. Something I should be remembering."

Sam studied her profile, her long brown lashes, her full lips. "Like what?"

"I don't know. Like…could it be that I saw something I should recognize, but just can't remember?"

"Yes. It's possible. You'd been drugged, you were scared. It's only natural you would miss things or not be able to remember."

With a sigh, Kaycee shook her head, then squeezed her temples between her fingers. "I know it's those pictures. I just can't remember anything specific about them."

"It will come, darlin'. Just give it time."

His gaze wandered lower, over her slim neck and down to her breasts. Her nipples poked through the fabric like hard little marbles begging to be suckled. His blood heated as he imagined feasting on those perfect mounds. She would fill his hands and he'd still have some left over.

His fingers splayed against her abdomen, flexing and sinking slightly into the soft flesh of her stomach. He heard her shallow intake of breath and glanced back up at her face. Her cheeks were flushed, her eyes ablaze.

Without thinking, he leaned closer so his nose could brush against the hairline at her temple. Her body stiffened, then relaxed as he feathered his lips across her temple. What was it about her that made him so weak, so…desperate to have her in his arms?

"Still scared?" he whispered, and she shook her head.

Her tongue flicked out to lick at her lips, and for a second he stopped breathing. This is what he'd felt earlier when he'd been looking for her and Tyler. He knew Tyler was aroused, knew what they were probably doing, but he'd searched for them anyway. If he fucked her, Tyler would know. It would wake him.

His lips moved lower, grazing along her cheek. Her breathing grew short, shallow. She was as turned on as he was. He could feel it, smell it.

"Do you have any idea how much I want you?" Sam whispered.

She swallowed and turned her face toward his. Her eyes were troubled, confused, but at the same time full of desire. The same desire raging through his veins. Raising his hand, he brushed his thumb along her jawline, watching as the moonlight reflected in the depths of her wide eyes.

God, she was beautiful.

"I've never met men like you," she whispered. "It scares me, Sam. The desire I feel for both of you."

He nodded in agreement as his hand slipped behind her head, his fingers clenching at the back of her neck. He wanted to kiss her, taste her, touch every inch of her body so badly he ached from it. Pulling her to him, he brushed his lips across hers, his gaze watching her closely. Maybe she was the one -- just maybe she was the woman who would complete him and Tyler.

His lips touched hers again, tentatively, gently. They were soft, yielding as he licked his tongue along the seam. Her mouth parted on a sigh and he slipped his tongue inside. She tasted of mint and cream, her tongue like warm velvet as it stroked along his, igniting his blood, fueling his need for more.

He moved over her, one thigh sliding between hers to rub along her pussy. She moaned, lifting her leg over his and fitting his thigh more firmly against her. Her arms lifted to encircle his neck as he deepened the kiss, demanding more from her as his tongue plundered inside the hot recesses of her mouth.

Every inch of his flesh tingled, pulsed to life as she melted beneath his touch, moaned into his mouth. His fingers slid lower to cup her ass and rock her against his thigh. Her response to him fueled his own desire until it became a raging fire quickly threatening to consume them both. All the anger and frustration he'd felt earlier, all the pent-up lust came rushing forward, intensifying the need to be buried inside her -- to claim her and make her theirs.

"Kaycee," he whispered as he broke away from her mouth and moved to place light, nibbling kisses along her neck.

She moaned, tilting her head to the side, allowing him better access. His teeth scraped across her flesh, and she shuddered in his arms. One of her hands slid along his chest, exploring his pecs and brushing her thumb across his nipple. A tremor raced up his back, making his cock hard as a rock and his balls tighten painfully.

Did she have any idea at all what she was doing to him? What she made him want to do to her?

"There's no turning back, Kaycee," he whispered in her ear as he moved his palm up to cup a firm breast through her tank top. They filled his hands perfectly and her moan was all the encouragement he needed to continue. "Once you're with me, you're with Tyler, too. He'll wait for you to make the move, but if it's not what you want, say so now. Tell me before I go too far and can't stop."

Kaycee trembled at Sam's softly spoken warning. He was giving her a chance to turn him away, to tell him no, but she didn't want to. She couldn't. She was too out of control, too far gone.

Pulling away from her, Sam moved to his knees, tugging her up with him. He grasped her wrists, holding them over her head, and she gasped at the forceful way he handled her. His gaze bored intently into hers, branding her, but she couldn't look away.

"Leave them there," he ordered.

He let go and she held them steady, watching, mesmerized, as he gripped the edge of her tank top and lifted it over her head. His gaze remained glued to her breasts as he dropped the top to the floor, forgotten.

"Lie back," he ordered again and she could do nothing more than comply. "Grip the headboard."

Desire flared in her eyes at his rough command. Her fingers gripped the headboard as Sam tugged at her pants and panties, quickly ridding her body of the garments. He couldn't take his eyes off her as his palms slowly slid along her. She was so beautiful.

He bent one of her knees, his lips placing a soft kiss on the inside of the sensitive skin. His mouth moved upward ever so slowly, his teeth nipping at the inside of her thigh as he worked ever closer to her wet, aching pussy.

She let her other leg fall to the side, opening herself up to him and his sensual kisses. He murmured his approval against her mound and she bucked her hips, wanting more, making his own body tremble in response. She made him crazy, but he was determined to take things slow, to make it last.

His tongue licked slowly up her slit and she gasped, desperate now for a more firm touch. Juices poured from her vagina and he lapped them up greedily.

"So sweet," he whispered. "So fucking sweet."

Her head tossed back and forth as she twisted and squirmed, forcing her pussy harder against his mouth. He was driving her mad, making her crazy.

"Sam," she sighed. "Oh, Sam."

"Give me more of your cream, Kaycee. Fill my mouth with it."

Sam thrust his tongue into her dripping channel and she cried out loudly into the quiet room. Her fingers tightened around the spindles of the headboard, her nails biting into the flesh of her palms. She'd never had a man talk to her like that. Command something of her. His voice was raw, sexual, caressing her like a hand; it did things to her she never imagined it would.

She felt herself falling, tumbling toward that elusive crest. Every part of her tensed and she groaned, lifting her hips from the bed. Sam's hand pushed her back down, his fingers flexing against her lower stomach. She moaned, fighting against him as she struggled to keep her sanity.

Sam pulled back slightly, his teeth nibbling along her labia and she almost sobbed at the loss. "No," she choked. "No, Sam. Don't stop."

"I'm not stopping," he murmured. "I'm never stopping."

The tip of his tongue circled her clit and she shuddered, gasping for air.

"God, you're incredible," he whispered. "Look at me."

She opened her eyes and stared down at him. His face was still between her legs, his mouth hovered directly over her screaming clit, his lips and chin wet with her juices. He used his stubble covered chin to brush across her clit, making her gasp. His intense, fiery stare left her breathless, and her heart pounded furiously out of control. He was driving her nuts -- insane.

His face lowered, his gaze still locked on hers through his lashes and she swallowed, knowing the second his mouth touched her, she'd shatter. His lips opened over her pulsing clit and she held her breath. Time moved in slow motion as he softly blew warm air against her. She bucked and hissed, hungry for more -- so much more. Warm lips circled her and he suckled at the swollen bud gently, sending her careening out of control.

Her hips lifted as she screamed out her release, but Sam shoved her back down, holding her still while his mouth greedily ate at her, drawing even more out of her. She whimpered as wave after intense wave rushed through her, heating her, shattering her until she thought she'd die from it.

She shook her head, fighting against his hold as his tongue flicked across her now overly sensitized nub. Her eyes closed, and she felt him move away from her, but she was drained, weak, she couldn't open them to see where he went.

"Sam?" she sighed.

"I'm still here," he replied roughly and she heard the distinct sound of a zipper being lowered.

Opening her eyes, she watched as he lowered his jeans, then his boxers, exposing a massive cock. Long and thick with a purple head staring back at her and black hair curling around the base. She drew in a deep breath and felt herself getting wetter. Felt her pussy clench in hunger. His fingers gripped the base and squeezed.

"Last chance, Kaycee," he said and her stare shot to his.

Would he really walk away if she told him to? With a shake of her head, she realized she didn't want him to. She wanted him inside her -- filling her, making her scream.

He moved back between her legs and bent over her, a hand on either side of her shoulders. "What do you want, Kaycee?" he asked, and bent to lick across her hard nipple.

She whimpered, then bit down on her lower lip. She'd never talked during sex. Never met a man that made her feel like she wanted to. But Sam. His hot mouth engulfed her breast and she moaned, arching her back.

"Tell me," he murmured around the tip. "Tell me you want me, Kaycee, because God help me, I can't leave now."

"I want you," she whispered, then louder, "Oh, please, Sam. I want you."

With a deep growl of satisfaction, he settled the head of his cock at her weeping entrance, then thrust forward, filling her with one powerfully strong thrust. She gasped and tried to scoot away, the shock of his initial thrust almost too overwhelming. He moaned, closing his eyes tight as he pressed his forehead to hers.

"Son of a bitch, you're tight," he growled. "Hold still, Kaycee. Please. Or I'll hurt you."

She stilled instantly, letting her hands move to his shoulders. She could feel the tension in his body as he struggled to hold still. He pulled back slightly, then pushed back in, and she gasped as she realized he still wasn't fully inside her. Again, he pulled back, gently pressing forward, stretching her resisting walls. Kaycee moaned as the slight bite of pain morphed into pleasure unlike anything she could imagine.

God, sex had never been like this for her and she felt herself getting wetter, felt her juices coat his cock as he slid deeper.

"Oh, fuck," he groaned as he pressed balls deep, his pelvis brushing gently against her clit.

Kaycee could hardly breathe it felt so good. She lifted a leg to circle his hip and Sam hissed through his teeth, his hand instantly moving to her hip to hold her still.

"God, darlin', don't move," he murmured against her lips. "You feel so good," he sighed. "So damn good."

His lips covered hers, his tongue seeking entrance. She opened her mouth, allowing him inside, her moan of delight becoming lost in his kiss. Slowly, he began to move, pulling out, then gently pushing back in. Her pussy stretched around him as he pressed forward, then gripped and clenched around his shaft as he pulled back.

His hold loosened on her hip and she began to move with him, lifting her hips to meet his slow deep thrusts.

"That's it, darlin'," he purred and she shuddered from head to toe at his deep, sexy drawl.

His movements increased, became faster, harder, deeper. She lifted her other leg and Sam reached beneath it to throw it over his shoulder. It brought him impossibly deep and she cried out as his pounding thrusts hit her cervix. His pelvis brushed against her clit relentlessly, sending sparks of pleasure to every part of her body.

"Sam," she screamed as her climax neared. Her stomach tensed, her hips jerked in reflex, wanting more, needing more. "Please. Oh, God."

He twisted his hips, pounding even harder, and she erupted into a mass of stinging rapture. Light exploded behind her eyes as her orgasm raced through her, making her scream out her release.

Sam gritted his teeth, closing his eyes against the feel of her pussy as it clamped down on his cock. He could feel every pulse of her channel, every wave as it raced through her. Her pussy squeezed at his shaft, taking everything he gave and sucking the life from his balls. With a shout of his own, he pressed deep, emptying his seed deep into her hot channel.

"Son of a bitch," he growled, realizing he'd lost his control and come inside her. "I'm so sorry, baby."

Kaycee sighed and opened her eyes to glance up at him dreamily. "What? Sorry for what?"

He swallowed. "I didn't use a condom."

She frowned slightly, then her lips twitched into a satisfied, kitten-like smile. "I take the shot. It's fine."

Relief washed through him, but part of him -- some small part -- felt disappointment. There would be no chance of pregnancy, no reason to try and hold her to them if she decided she wanted to run.

"Please tell me your brother is like you."

Sam glanced down at her in surprise. There was no jealousy at the thought of her being with Tyler. She'd only been with him. She hadn't been with his brother or the two of them together. He refused to get his hopes up, refused to think of her as theirs just yet.

"He's exactly like me." Leaning down, he brushed his mouth across hers, enjoying her sigh as it blew across his lips.

She shook her head. "I've never done the two men thing, Sam. Honestly, it scares me."

Sam swallowed and let her leg fall back to the bed. With his palm he cupped her cheek and placed a gentle kiss on her brow. "I know. But I promise we would never hurt you and we'll make sure you're ready. Prepared."

"How do you do it? One in my pussy, the other in my ass? Would that actually work?"

Sam's cock hardened at the mere mention of sharing her with his brother and he groaned. "Now's probably not the best time to talk about this, Kaycee. Talk like that tends to turn me on."

She smiled slightly, then leaned up to nibble along his jawline. "What about Tyler?" she whispered. "How...how is this done?"

He raised a brow, tilting his head slightly to give her better access. God, she was sweet, tentative...almost innocent.

"You go to Tyler when you're ready to go to Tyler," he murmured.

"Tyler won't come to me?"

"Not if you slept with me first." He shifted slightly, pushing his thick cock deeper into her hot sheath, and she moaned. "He'll wait for you to make the first move. Do you have any idea what thinking about you with Tyler does to me?"

Sam pulled back till only the head of his shaft was inside her, then slowly pushed back in, moaning as every inch of his cock slid along her slick pussy.

"Oh, God." She gulped.

"Like that, darlin'?" he purred, then did it again, swallowing his own groan of pleasure as her walls rippled around him.

"Yes," she whispered, her nails digging into his back, her hips lifting to rotate against his.

This time he did groan as he thrust again, deeper. "God, Kaycee. You're going to drive me fucking insane," he growled, then covered her lips with his, swallowing her moans.

* * *

He stood in his living room staring at a picture of Kaycee. Her hair was up, her eyes laughing. It was from the spring *Vogue* shoot in Miami. She'd looked so good that day, so happy.

Setting the picture on the coffee table, he drew his finger along her cheek, imagining it was her flesh beneath his touch and not the cold paper. She was all he'd ever wanted from the first day he'd met her. But she'd turned him down, actually grimaced at his kiss. She claimed he'd been rough, hurt her. He hadn't come anywhere near to hurting her yet.

He'd underestimated her, that's all. Next time he'd know better. Next time, she wouldn't get away.

She would be his again soon. Very soon.

Chapter Six

Kaycee walked into the kitchen early the next morning almost hesitantly. Sam had already headed out to the barn, leaving her alone in the house with Tyler. In the back of her mind she wondered if he'd done that on purpose. That maybe he hoped she'd sleep with Tyler today.

Her body hummed at the idea, even though it also screamed from the battering she'd received from Sam the night before. Damn, that man had stamina. Had she really come four times? There were times in the past she'd never come at all, only faked it so her lover would hurry and finish, then leave her alone to try and sleep it off.

With a sigh, she rounded the fireplace and decided to face this head on. Would he know? She spotted him at the kitchen table, a cup of coffee in his hand, the morning paper spread before him. He wore a denim shirt, just a few shades lighter than his jeans. The sleeves were rolled up, showing off his thick, muscular forearms. She'd never paid much attention to a guy's forearms but for some reason she thought his and Sam's were the sexiest she'd ever seen and couldn't stop looking. Firm and corded, they made her shiver every time she saw them.

Lifting her eyes, she met Tyler's and inwardly flinched. Yep, he knew. The hunger blazing in his eyes was a mirror image of Sam's last night. Sam said he would know, but the reality of it was so much more unnerving. Was he angry? Hurt?

"Good morning."

His deep, booming voice floated across the room, smoothing over her skin like a caress. God, she was screwed.

His lips twitched slightly and the hunger in his deep blue gaze shifted to amusement. "Sleep well?"

The heat of a blush moved over her cheeks. How had this happened so fast? It scared the hell out of her. What if this was only the damsel falling for her protectors? What if it wasn't real?

"As well as can be expected, I suppose." She shrugged and headed to the coffee pot to get some much needed caffeine in her system. "How did you sleep?"

"Not well. I usually don't when Sam is fucking just a few feet away from me."

She gasped and turned to stare at him in shock. "God, Tyler. Do you have to just lay it out there like that?" Her eyes closed on a groan. There she went, yapping without thinking again.

"Yes. I do." He set down his paper and shifted in his chair to face her. "Are you sure about this, Kaycee? If not, it's my fault. I've been trying to convince Sam since I met you that you were the one for us." He stood and walked toward her, his gait strong, sure, and so damn sexy. "I know it's weird. And it's unorthodox." Kaycee nodded, making Tyler smile slightly. "But it can also be amazing. Two men putting you first. Your needs first. Two men who would love you beyond reason."

"But is it really love?" she whispered. "What if it's not, Tyler? What if it turns out to be nothing more than the situation we're in?"

"I don't believe that, Kaycee." He brushed the back of his fingers along her cheek, making her tremble. "And I think if you look deep inside…neither would you."

He winked, then turned to leave the room. "I left you some eggs and bacon in the microwave if you want them. I'm going to head to my office and get some paperwork done."

Kaycee watched him go with a heavy heart, her gaze glued to his wide back. She wasn't sure what she'd expected, but that certainly hadn't been it. He seemed accepting of the whole thing -- understanding. She'd slept with his brother for crying out loud, after she'd dry humped Tyler just a few hours before.

"This is nuts," she grumbled as she hit the button on the microwave, warming her breakfast. "No, Kaycee. What's nuts is that you want to go to that office and have Tyler fuck you on his desk." She slammed her coffee cup down on the counter. She had a terrible feeling her life would never be normal again.

Tyler sat in his office, blindly staring at the bills. He couldn't get his mind off Kaycee's screams from the night before. He'd heard her. Heard every last moan and yell as Sam had brought her to orgasm four fucking times.

He dropped his head in his hands. They'd ruined their past relationships by rushing things. This time, they'd do it right. This time, he'd wait for her. But damn, he wanted her. He'd wanted to burst into that bedroom and join them, show her what it would be like with the two of them. But he and his brother had decided if it did happen, they would have to wait for her to make the move toward the second brother.

She knew what they needed. She knew if one wanted her, so did the other. She knew what they would want from her, but it would have to be her choice. Tyler wouldn't seduce her. But God help him, he wanted to.

"I'm not sure I can wait," he mumbled.

"Wait for what?"

He jerked his head up and saw Kaycee standing in the doorway, two cups of steaming coffee in her hands. She shrugged. "I was lonely. Mind if I join you?"

"No," he said, shaking his head.

She strolled forward and he admired her jeans and pink turtleneck. The color suited her complexion and made her eyes sparkle. He took the cup she handed him and studied her concerned frown.

"What's wrong?" he asked. "There's more bothering you than me and Sam."

She nodded, then took the seat on the other side of the desk. "There were pictures of me in his..." She waved her hand. "Lair, I guess for a lack of a better word."

Tyler's lips twitched. "Yeah. Lots of them."

"There was something about those pictures, Tyler. Something I know I should have noticed, but I can't remember. You said they cleaned it out. Do they still have them?"

"Yes. They're in with the other evidence. There weren't any fingerprints, though. They've already been checked."

She shook her head. "It's not fingerprints. It's the pictures themselves. I need to see them. Can we do that?"

Tyler nodded. "Sure. I'll have Barreck send them over."

"Good," she said, then took a sip of her coffee, studying him thoughtfully. "How did you and Sam get involved with the FBI?"

Taking a deep breath, Tyler sat back in his chair. They hadn't told her all of it yet, but he supposed now was as good a time as any. "Our father was an agent. He specialized in missing persons. One night Sam and I picked up a sweater belonging to a missing child. We both touched it, then connected with her." Kaycee's eyes widened slightly, but she remained silent, allowing him to continue. "We were eight. Terrified by what we were seeing. My mother wanted to stop us, but as soon as my father realized what was happening, he encouraged us to stay with her. You see, my father had worked with registered psychics before and knew what was happening more than we did."

"You can't be serious."

"I'm dead serious." Tyler leaned forward, putting his elbows on the desk. "He had you tied to a gurney. You used your teeth to loosen the knotted ropes around your wrists, then threw up the second you got up." Her eyes widened, but he continued. "You tried to help her, tried to get her free, but she was chained and you couldn't get them undone. She told you he called her Kaycee. You hit him with a bat first, then you stabbed him. The feel of the blood on your hand repulsed you. You fought your way out, Kaycee, with him on your tail the whole way. You could hear him breathing, his curses. You could smell him."

She shook her head, her astonished gaze locked on his. "How?"

"They found your scarf. Tyler and I touched it and connected with you. We stayed with you until you fell in front of the police car."

"Do you still have the scarf?" she asked softly.

"It's with evidence. But I can get it back for you."

She sat there, her confused gaze watching him, studying him, her mind working through it all. "Are you still connected to me? Can you still see what I see?"

He shook his head. "It only works if we're both touching something of yours."

"What happens when you both touch me? Will you connect with me?"

"It doesn't work that way. It doesn't happen every time we both touch something. We have to relax. We have to *allow* it to come through."

"But you could. You could both touch…" she shrugged. "My sweater or my hospital gown while I'm standing next to you and you would see what I see? Feel what I feel?"

After a second's hesitation, Tyler nodded.

Her eyes narrowed and Tyler braced himself for the anger he knew was coming. "So you knew before I ever came here. You knew at the hospital I was attracted to you both?"

This time, Tyler glanced toward the desk and nodded once.

"You son of a bitch!"

Guilt raced through him. He knew what she must be thinking and in part she was right. Raising his gaze, he noticed a furious Sam standing in the doorway to his office. Apparently, he'd come in from the barn and caught the tail end of their conversation. And he wasn't happy.

"You knew. You saw an opportunity to take advantage."

Tyler shook his head. "No. That's not it, Kaycee."

"The hell it's not!"

She stood and stormed from the room, shoving a startled Sam out of her way.

"What the hell just happened?" Sam growled, then glared at him with narrowed eyes. "You fucking told her."

"Stay out of this, Sam. It's my screw up, I'll fix it."

"You better fucking fix it," Sam snapped, but Tyler ignored him, instead heading down the hall to find Kaycee.

He heard the front door slam, then froze in his tracks. Damn it, she shouldn't be outside. Rushing to the door, he flung it open, then spotted her rushing across the field toward the barn. He took off after her at a run, his heart pounding furiously in his chest. God, he'd screwed up. He should have lied. He could have handled that one question so much better.

Throwing open the barn doors, he stood in the entryway, allowing his eyes to become accustomed to the dim interior.

"Kaycee," he called, then remained quiet, listening for any sign of where she was. He heard nothing and his heart stopped. "Damn it, Kaycee, answer me. If you don't I'm going to assume he has you and I'm going to tear this barn apart beam by beam until I find you."

"Just go away, Tyler."

Her voice came from the stall at the farthest end and he sighed in relief. "We need to talk about this."

"There's nothing to talk about," she snapped. "You felt that I was attracted to the two of you and you took advantage. You jumped at the chance to share me."

He opened the stall door and glared at her as she leaned against the back wall, her eyes glowing, her breasts heaving in anger. "That's not it, damn it," he snarled. "Yes, we knew you were attracted to us. But we didn't bring you here because of that. Hell, Sam even fought me on it." He heaved a sigh, waving his hand toward the house. "Bringing you here was my idea because I felt something when I connected with you. Something I've never felt before."

He stepped toward her cautiously, slowly, watching her for any sign she might be giving in.

"You've had other women who were attracted to both of you," she accused.

"Yes. But it wasn't right. Maybe they only thought they were attracted. Maybe it was the idea that seemed fascinating, but the reality scared them off. But you're different." He put his hand on the stall by her head and leaned forward slightly. Her eyes darkened in desire and her skin flushed. Even her breathing changed. "I can touch you and get the same spark of heat in your gaze you give Sam when he touches you. To you, we're equal. You don't want one more than the other." He leaned even closer. Close enough to smell the coffee on her breath as it blew across his lips. His free hand raised to cup her neck as his thumb tilted up her chin. "It was never that way with the others. Sam and I would both be attracted, but they always wanted one of us more than the other. They never desired us equally. Only the woman who's meant to be ours would react to us the same. Like you, Kaycee."

His thumb swiped across her lower lip, then tugged downward, making them part. "I bet you're wet now, aren't you? As wet as you were with Sam?"

She swallowed, her confused and aroused gaze glued to his.

He shook his head, cursing himself for his lack of control. "I swore I'd wait for you, but I can't --"

Her fingers fisted in his shirt, tugging him those last few inches until his lips captured hers in a kiss that held all the hunger he felt raging through him. His tongue thrust into her mouth, plundering, demanding a response. And she gave him one. One that stole the very breath from his lungs. He growled into her mouth, sucking greedily at her tongue and lips until she clung to him, her fingers fisting in his shirt, her body sliding down the wall.

With a groan, he put his hands at her waist, holding her up as he pressed her more firmly against the wall. He bent his knees slightly and let his hard cock settle within the soft vee of her thighs and she moaned, wiggling against him enticingly. God, she was driving him insane.

His fingers worked frantically to free the button of her jeans. Once unzipped, he shoved them to her ankles, moving back slightly so she could kick them aside. She stared up at him, her eyes full of hungry desire, her mouth swollen and wet from his kiss. Letting his gaze wander down her body, he lifted the hem of her shirt, admiring her pink thong.

His palm slid around to smooth over her ass, and she sighed, moving her hips out from the wall. "Those are nice," he whispered. "But they've got to fucking go."

Grabbing them, he pushed them down as well, squatting to remove them from around her ankles. In this position, her pussy was right at his face. He could smell her, smell her arousal, and God, she smelled like heaven. With pressure on the inside of her thighs, he ordered. "Spread your legs."

She did and he leaned between them, sliding his tongue through the thick juices coating her labia. She gasped, burying her fingers in his hair, trying to pull him closer. She tasted so good. Like honey. Musky honey. He ate his fill. Licking, delving, lapping at every drop leaking from her hot walls.

Her fingers clenched in his scalp; her soft, moaning pleas filled his ears and ran hot through his veins. He was out of his mind with wanting her. All night he'd listened to those same mewling sounds, those same cries of passion, and he'd nearly lost it. Nearly broke down the bedroom door so he could join them, burying his cock in her pussy like he knew Sam was.

He'd felt her heat just like Sam did. He'd felt the choke hold her tight walls had on Sam's cock, felt her heat seeping into him like a warm fire.

Kaycee squealed as Tyler's tongue thrust into her pulsing walls. God help her. He had her so wild and he'd been right -- she did want him as bad as she wanted Sam. She growled and jerked her hips toward his face. God, he was good at this. They both were and heaven help her, she was about to come.

"Tyler," she groaned, but he pulled away, denying her what she so desperately wanted.

He stood up before her, his hands working his jeans and boxers off. With a growl, he put his hands under her hips and lifted her, positioning the head of his cock at her weeping entrance. The desire blazed hot in his gaze and she knew hers matched it -- maybe even surpassed it. Cream leaked from her core to coat the head of his shaft as he pressed forward just a little.

"Say it," he commanded and she knew instinctively what he wanted to hear.

"Damn it, Tyler. Fuck me," she growled, then screamed as he pressed forward, burying himself deep.

He was as big as Sam, maybe bigger if the tearing pain she felt was any indication. She tensed, then whimpered as he pulled out, then pressed forward again, this time going deeper. His pelvis brushed against her clit and she shuddered, wiggling her hips.

"Ah, fuck yeah," he groaned low in his chest as he thrust harder, making her gasp for air and struggle to accommodate him.

She was still sore, still swollen from last night, but that didn't stop her need to feel Tyler pounding into her harder -- making her feel the same mind-numbing pleasure that Sam had. Her body tensed and her pussy gripped his cock harder, milking him.

"Tyler," she squealed and everything around her blurred.

Her pussy rippled along his length, sucking at him as she erupted into a ball of screaming pleasure. Her nails dug into his shoulder, holding tight as he tilted her hips and ground his pelvis against her clit. She gasped, then screamed as another more powerful orgasm raced through her.

"Oh, God. Tyler," she yelled, shaking her head, fighting against the rapture threatening to make her pass out.

With a shout of his own, Tyler came as well, emptying his hot seed into her passage with a sharp jerk of his hips. She sagged against the wall, her hands still holding tight to his shoulders.

"What the hell just happened?" she gasped, her breathing still harsh and erratic. "Wasn't I supposed to be mad at you?"

Tyler buried his face in her neck, his hot breath sending ripples of prickly desire down her spine. Oh, God. She was going to get horny all over again if she didn't stop him. His lips nipped at the sensitive spot behind her ear and she sighed, shifting her hips against his.

"Don't move, Kaycee," he groaned and gripped her waist. "If that's what it's like when you're mad, baby, you can get mad at me all you want to."

The heat of a blush moved over her cheeks. "I have to be out of my mind. That attacker made me addle-minded."

Tyler chuckled, then leaned back looking at her face. But his hips. Oh, God, his hips pressed her back against the wall, lodging that amazing cock even deeper and she swallowed.

"I'm still mad at you," she growled, only half meaning it.

His lips spread into a soft smile and he leaned down to brush them across hers. It was such a sensual kiss, different from the wild, uninhibited fuck they'd just experienced.

"And I'm still crazy about you."

He said it right up against her mouth where every movement of his lips brushed across hers and she shivered from head to toe. God, help her. These two were going to turn her to mush.

Chapter Seven

"Feeling better?"

Kaycee blinked and turned her gaze from the horses in the coral to Sam. He looked handsome in his denim jacket and low-riding Stetson; she had to grab the fence railing to keep from swooning. The hat shadowed his eyes, making it difficult to see what he was thinking, but he seemed relaxed as he placed one booted foot along the bottom rung, and let his forearms drape across the top one, his hands clasped.

"Yeah. I guess I just freaked out for a second. Your and Tyler's ability is a bit much to swallow."

Sam's lips twitched. "Yeah, I know. It is for us too at times." He shrugged. "But we've learned to live with it. Control it."

She turned back to the fence and rested her arms along the top, her gaze following a small colt as it skipped around the coral. Tyler stood at the far end with two other ranch hands repairing the far gate. Did Sam know what had happened between her and Tyler? Should she tell him? Say something? She didn't have a clue how to handle this.

"I know you fucked Tyler."

Kaycee rolled her eyes, her face heating in embarrassment. "God, do you have to be so crude?"

Sam chuckled deep in his chest. "Sorry. It's okay, Kaycee. You'll" -- he waved his hand -- "make love to him and you'll make love to me."

"This doesn't bother you?" she asked.

"Why would it? He wants you just as much as I do."

"But what if a stranger wanted me as much?"

He frowned. "Now that would be different."

She turned to face him, not understanding that logic at all. A breeze blew her hair across her face and she brushed it aside in growing agitation. "Why?"

"Because Tyler is me. A stranger's not."

Putting her hand on her hip, she glared. "Sam, that makes no sense at all."

"I know it doesn't, but that's the way it is. We're the same soul, Kaycee. When he hurts, I hurt. When I love, he loves. It's the way we've always been and the way we always will be. For Tyler to touch you, it's as if I touched you." He grinned. "Corny as it sounds."

She snorted. "Well, you got the corny right."

Sam chuckled and adjusted his Stetson, pushing it back slightly. "Tyler requested those pictures for you."

She nodded and turned her gaze back to the horse, squinting as the sun broke through from behind the thick, puffy clouds.

"Why did you want to see them?"

"Do you remember last night when I told you there was something I know I'm missing?"

"Yeah."

"It was the pictures. There's something familiar about the pictures, but I can't remember enough about them. So I wanted to see them."

"As soon as Barreck signs them out he's going to overnight them. There's lots of paperwork involved for the paper trail so the whole process will take a day or two."

She sighed, hoping if she saw the snapshots, she would figure it out. As much as she enjoyed spending time with Sam and Tyler, she did miss certain aspects of her life. Friends, for one. She hadn't been able to talk to her assistant, Jordan, for days. And she could certainly use a friend right now. Someone to help her work through this attraction she had toward both men.

Unfortunately, they kept her sequestered. Truthfully, she understood why. She didn't want to be killed any more than they wanted it, but she couldn't stay hidden forever. She would go nuts. She needed friends, she needed movies, she needed nights out.

"Can we go out or something, Sam?" she asked.

He quirked an eyebrow. "You mean like a date?"

She jerked her head around and almost giggled at his stunned expression. "Not really a date. Just…" She shrugged.

"You're going stir crazy, aren't you?" he asked, one corner of his lips lifting in a slight grin.

"A little."

"I know it can get boring out here sometimes, but I'm not sure it would be a good idea to be parading you around town. You're too high profile and the papers would have a field day if they recognized you. How about we do this?"

He turned and leaned his back against the fence. Her gaze immediately dropped to his thick chest and trim waist, surrounded by a brown leather belt and silver belt buckle. That one was definitely all cowboy.

"What?" she asked, almost breathlessly as her gaze moved back to his heavenly blue eyes. They watched her with a hint of amusement, but she didn't miss the dark desire simmering just beyond the blue of his orbs.

"A movie night. There's a media room in the basement. We can make popcorn, have a few drinks." He wiggled his eyebrow. "Make out in the back row."

She couldn't stop the nervous giggle or the butterflies that instantly jumped to life in her stomach at the thought of kissing Sam. "What movies do you have?"

Sam snorted. "Tyler is a movie fanatic. There's probably hundreds of DVD's down there. But if we don't have anything you like, I can always run to town and pick something up."

She shrugged one shoulder, her mind constantly flipping back to kissing Sam in the back row, imagining what his hands would do to her in the dark confines of the media room. And would Tyler join them? What would it be like to have both of them kissing her? "Sounds like a plan."

"Good. Media room is down the stairs and to the right, at the end of the hall. Pick something out and as soon as we're done here, I'll make us some popcorn. You like it buttery?"

I'd like you buttery.

She licked her lips, imagining butter smeared all over Sam's impressive chest. Oh, yeah, she would definitely like it buttery.

He's talking about the popcorn, idiot.

Did he know what she was thinking? What she wanted again after only screwing Tyler just a few hours ago? She would bet he did if the lust shining in his gaze was any indication. Her heart fluttered as the heat of a blush moved up her cheeks. "I love buttered popcorn," she whispered.

Then with a deep breath, she turned to head back to the house. She could feel his gaze on her back, boring a hole into her the entire way and she fought the urge to turn and look at him. The idea of him and Tyler both making love to her was becoming more and more intriguing. But could she actually go through with it, or would she be like all the others? Would she run from them, too?

* * *

He strolled into the hospital, glancing around. He still wasn't sure how he was going to go about this, until his stare landed on a pretty nurse behind the nurse's station. With a slight smile, he moved forward and rested his elbows against the countertop, leaning forward slightly.

"Good morning," he said.

The nurse glanced up at him and her eyes widened in surprise just before her lips spread into a welcoming smile.

"Good morning. Can I help you?"

He glanced around the nurse's station at the University of Tennessee Hospital. Kaycee had been injured, so it hadn't been difficult to determine they would take her here.

His gaze shifted back to the nurse, who watched him expectantly from her position on the stool. She wore her brown hair pinned back from her face, accentuating her long, graceful neck. His cock twitched behind the zipper of his pants as he noticed just how much her neck reminded him of Kaycee's.

"Yes…" He dropped his gaze to look at her badge. "Melissa. I'm here to see Kaycee Alcott. I understand she was brought here after her unfortunate accident."

"Oh, yes. The model." Melissa nodded, then turned to click her pretty pink nails across a computer keyboard. She watched him through her lashes and he gave her his best smile. He knew he oozed charm -- knew women found him attractive and he used it to his advantage.

"Do you know her personally?" Melissa asked.

"Yes. I've worked with her numerous times. She's one of my favorite models. Has anyone told you how much you look like her?"

A slight flush moved over her cheeks and a shy smile pulled at her full lips. "A few." She giggled. "Do you work in the modeling industry?"

"Yes. For almost fifteen years now." He reached into his pocket and handed a card to her across the counter -- the one proclaiming him a fashion photographer. "I'm quite good at picking out future supermodels."

She studied his card, then smiled up at him, her eyes full of sparkle and excitement. She was definitely pretty, but not as pretty as Kaycee. She lacked that bone structure, that certain lift to the corner of her eyes. Her gaze flicked back to the screen. "I'm so sorry, but you missed her. She checked out several days ago."

"That must have been why she was trying to call me, but I'm afraid my cell has been giving me problems. It doesn't by any chance say who checked her out, does it?"

The nurse glanced around nervously. "I really shouldn't be telling you this, but…"

She licked her lips and leaned closer. He did as well, meeting her halfway across the counter so she could whisper. Her musky perfume invaded his nose, and he held his breath. He hated women who loaded themselves down with perfume. Kaycee never did that. She smelled heavenly without it.

"A Tyler Warren checked her out. All her medical bills were sent to the FBI."

He raised an eyebrow. So the FBI had her. Didn't surprise him really. Now he just had to find out where this Tyler Warren was. "Does it give an address by any chance? I have the proofs from her last shoot and I'm sure she's anxious to see them." He pulled a magazine from his jacket pocket. Unrolling it, he placed it on the counter between them. With the tip of his finger, he tapped at Kaycee's bikini-clad body on the cover. "She also made the cover of *Sports Illustrated*. She doesn't know yet and I'd really like to surprise her with the news."

She pushed back from the counter, indecision clearly etched in her face. "You have beautiful eyes," he murmured, slightly changing his tactic. "Have dinner with me."

"Dinner?"

"Sure. Just you and me. We can talk about the possibility of a modeling future."

Her eyes widened and the rise and fall of her breasts increased with her excitement. "You think I could be a model?"

"Absolutely. Maybelline is looking for women just like you. Sophisticated, beautiful. Maybe you'll let me do some shots. I don't have all my equipment here, but I'm sure I can make do with the digital I have. If I can get an address, I can mail the proofs to Kaycee and stick around here for a day or two."

Biting her lip, she stared at the computer again. "It doesn't give an address. But I remember them saying something about a small town outside of Amarillo."

"Do you remember the name of the town?"

"No. But I could try to find out for you."

He smiled. "Excellent. What time do you get off?"

"Four."

"Perfect. I'll pick you up out front and we'll head out for an early dinner."

"I'd like that," she said, her smile spreading.

He walked away, his mind imaging all the things he'd do to her body. Let her tell her friends. The card and the name were fake, just like always. His cock twitched and hardened at the thought of the night ahead. She wasn't his norm, but that didn't matter anymore. What mattered most was getting Kaycee.

* * *

Kaycee dropped onto the soft leather couch that spanned the second row of their little media room. Heck of a room. It looked like a theater, with the large screen at the opposite end, red curtains flanking the sides as well as the other walls. There were no windows and the only lighting was the small sconces on the walls casting their soft glow around the room. The ceiling had been painted black with small pinholes allowing the soft light above the ceiling to shine through, creating a spectacular nighttime sky.

"You guys went all out with this place, didn't you?" she asked, her gaze still on the sparkling stars above.

Tyler and Sam both dropped to the couch, one on either side of her. They'd all changed into lounging pants and T-shirts.

Their hot flesh burned hers even through the soft cotton of their clothes as they both moved closer to her, pinning her between them like the lunchmeat in the middle of a Warren sandwich, and her heart skipped a beat.

Sam glanced up at the ceiling as well. "You think we went overboard?"

"No. It's beautiful."

"So are you," Tyler whispered in her ear, and her breath caught in her throat.

"I picked *The Matrix*. I hope that's okay," she blurted. Her nerves were jumping. One of them made her crazy; the two of them together were overwhelming her.

"Sorry, I didn't have any romantic comedies," Tyler murmured, his lips twitching in amusement, his eyes crinkling adorably, and her flesh warmed.

Yeah, right. Sure he was.

She shrugged. "I like *The Matrix*."

All she could think about was earlier in the barn. Tyler fucking her against the stall, his cock pounding into her over and over, filling her, stretching her. She turned her gaze to Sam, who lifted a bowl of popcorn from the chair beside their couch and turned to set it on her lap. His gaze met hers and lust sparked, darkening the blue of his eyes and making her shudder.

"I'm in the middle, so I hold the popcorn?" she asked, teasing him.

The bowl warmed her suddenly cold hands. Sam's slow, seductive grin warmed her pussy. Grabbing some, she popped a piece into her mouth, enjoying the salty, buttery taste, and turned to watch the screen as the movie flickered to life. The lights went out, leaving them in darkness except for the glow of the screen. Everything was controlled by the remote in Tyler's hand and she shook her head in amazement.

She'd seen some amazing houses in her career, had even been to the Playboy mansion. But there was something about this place, these two men, that made her feel at home, at peace. Could Tyler be right? Could she really be the one meant for them?

Glancing down, she noticed their thighs touching hers. The whole scene felt right, but a part of her was still concerned she wouldn't be able to go through with it. Sex with both of them? Hell, just one was more than a handful. What would she do with them both? But she couldn't deny her attraction -- the desire to touch them, kiss them. And not just one.

The movie progressed, each of them eating popcorn from the bowl, but she watched very little of the show. Instead, her mind kept playing out scenarios, sexual scenarios starring both her cowboys as they seduced her right here. Her fingers bumped Tyler's as he reached into the bowl for popcorn.

He lifted her hand, but kept his gaze on the screen as he slid each of her fingers into his warm mouth to lick off the salt and butter. Tingles ran the entire length of her spine and she turned her head to watch as each digit slid between his lips. His tongue circled them, licking them clean before moving on to the next one. He turned her hand to kiss her palm. His tongue flicked out to trace the lifeline and her stomach knotted into a tense ball.

"Tyler," she whispered without thinking, and he turned to stare at her, his gaze hot with desire.

Leaning over, he cupped the back of her head and pulled her lips to his. They were soft and warm, demanding as he deepened the kiss, invading her mouth with long, sensual swipes of his tongue.

"You taste like popcorn," he whispered, his lips spreading into a grin against hers.

"So do you."

"Let me taste," Sam murmured as he turned her toward him.

His kiss was gentler, more coaxing as his lips covered hers, swallowing her sigh of pleasure. Wow. Kissing the two of them at the same time was one of the most erotic things she'd ever felt and every part of her body pulsed to life. Especially her pussy. It leaked juices, soaking her lounging pants, and all they'd done was kiss her.

Tyler tugged at her hair, pulling her from Sam's kiss and turned her to once again accept his. "My turn again," he whispered, capturing her mouth in a kiss that stole her breath.

She whimpered, sagging toward the back of the couch, weak with lust and desire while Sam set the popcorn bowl on the floor. Sam's lips nibbled up the inside of her arm, softly biting at her flesh as he worked his way to her shoulder. Two warm palms, one Sam's and one Tyler's, slid under the hem of her shirt, feathering over sensitive flesh as they worked their way to her breasts.

Both cupped them, then brushed their thumbs across her nipples and she shuddered, heat burning straight through to her womb. It was amazing how they moved together, moved as one.

"Give me that mouth, Kaycee," Sam growled, and she broke away from Tyler and turned to let Sam feast on her lips.

God, this was insane. Her whole body burned for them, desired them, needed them. Tyler lifted her top, exposing her bare breasts. His teeth bit at a nipple and she gasped into Sam's mouth. Her breasts swelled, ached for more as Tyler licked and tugged at the hardened peaks, sending her need spiraling out of control.

Sam broke the kiss and helped Tyler lift her top over her head, tossing it to the darkened floor. Each of them removed their shirts as well and she gazed hungrily at their hard, tanned chests. Reaching out, she ran her palm over Tyler's pecs then up over his shoulders. His skin was smooth, hot to the touch, and his stare burned even hotter. Sliding her hand into his hair, she gripped his longer locks and tugged him to her for a kiss.

He tasted so good. The butter and salt mingled with his own flavor only made her hungry for more.

Sam gripped the waistband of her pants and tugged. "Lift up, darlin'."

She lifted her hips and he slid them off her weak, wobbly legs. The warm air of the room hit her pussy, and she moaned, spreading her legs.

"No underwear?" Sam teased as he pressed her thighs wider with his palms.

She shook her head, unsure why she'd decided to go without any. Had she wanted them to do this? Had a part of her known this would happen? Sam's lips worked a path up the inside of her thigh and she panted in quick, short breaths, desperate for the feel of his mouth on her aching mound.

Tyler moved to kiss her neck, working his way down to her breasts. She was on fire -- so on fire -- and she scooted to the edge of the seat to give Sam better access to her labia. He moaned his approval as his tongue slid along her slit, making her gasp.

"God, you taste good, darlin'," he purred from between her legs, his voice vibrating against her clit.

She couldn't speak. All she could do was hold on for dear life as Sam ate out her pussy, his tongue licking away the juices pouring from her vagina. Tyler removed his pants and straddled her hips, putting his long, thick cock directly in front of her face. One of his hands gripped the back of the couch, as the other gripped the base of his shaft, positioning his thick head at her lips.

"Lick it, baby. Take me in your sweet mouth."

His deep, sexy voice washed over her like warm honey and she opened her lips, twirling her tongue around the tip, then across the top, swiping at the precum glistening on the head. Tyler groaned, his fingers tightening around the base of his cock.

Between her legs, Sam separated her labia with his fingers, then swiped his tongue into her channel. She sighed, lifting her hips against his face as she opened her lips to engulf the head of Tyler's cock. He tasted so good, salty, and she sucked hard, pulling more of his salty cum to the tip. She licked at it with the flat of her tongue and his hips jerked.

"Oh, yeah, that's it, baby. Just like that."

Her mouth opened again, taking him farther inside this time. He was so thick her jaw ached, but she ignored it, instead focusing on the intense pleasure contorting his face. Sam flicked his tongue across her clit and her hips bucked uncontrollably, her moan vibrating along the velvety length of Tyler's shaft, making Tyler hiss through his clenched teeth.

"Keep that up, baby, and you'll get more than you bargained for."

Tyler's comment made her smile to herself. She was already getting more than she'd bargained for. Pressing his cock to his stomach, she traced her tongue up the long, thick vein running the underside from balls to tip. Sam slid two fingers into her dripping pussy and she almost came. Her walls pulsed around the invading digits, and her womb clenched tight. With a moan, she sucked at Tyler's balls.

"Damn," Tyler groaned. "She's fucking killing me." He moved away to sit on the couch beside her. "Get over here, Kaycee," he growled, tugging at her elbow.

Sam removed his fingers and helped her to straddle Tyler's lap. Positioning her hips over his shaft, Tyler gripped her waist and pulled down, impaling her with one powerful, deep thrust. She struggled for air, throwing her head back to gape at the ceiling above her. God, she felt full and so consumed she wanted to scream.

Her nails dug into Tyler's shoulder, leaving half moons on his skin as he rocked her hips front to back, his cock burrowing deeper with every movement of her hips. Sam moved behind her, pressing his chest to her back. She moaned, but a small part of her tensed in trepidation. She'd never let anyone take her in the ass. Is that what he had planned? Is that what he was preparing to do?

She felt his wet, warm fingers probing at the opening to her ass and she tensed, her hips stilling over Tyler's.

"Shhh, darlin'. I won't hurt you."

He slid one finger inside her tight anal passage and she gasped in shock.

"You're not ready for both of us yet," Sam whispered, as he added a second finger.

She shuddered as the sharp, biting pain turned to pleasure, hot searing pleasure that made her hips jerk, taking Tyler's cock and Sam's fingers even deeper. Tyler groaned and thrust his hips upward, hitting her cervix, and a ripple of intense heat ricocheted through her body.

"We'll do this first," Sam purred, thrusting his fingers in gentle counterpart to Tyler's cock. "Then we'll graduate to toys and butt plugs." She shuddered, imagining taking one of them with a plug stuck where Sam's fingers were. "Then both of us. Would you like that, Kaycee? Both of us fucking you at once?"

She swallowed, sighing as the pleasure-pain built deep inside her, radiating outward like a wave. Her ass burned, her pussy wept as both men took her to heights she never dreamed she'd feel. It was insane, but she had a feeling this was only the beginning -- the pleasure she felt now, no matter how intense, only scratched the surface of what they could show her.

"You're close, aren't you darlin'?" Sam purred.

With his other hand, he reached around and pinched her nipple, making her whimper. "Come all over his cock for me, Kaycee," Sam hissed, his fingers tugging at her engorged nipple. "Make him come so that my dick can get a taste of that tight, wet pussy."

Tyler gripped her hips, his fingers digging into her flesh, working her hips in a faster, harder rhythm. She screamed as pleasure raced through her limbs, tightening her womb. Her pussy clenched around Tyler's cock and he shouted, lifting her upward to shoot his cum deep into her channel. Her ass squeezed at Sam's fingers, rippling along his digits and increasing the rapture she felt eating her alive.

Before her throbs had even subsided, Tyler lifted her off his cock allowing Sam to thrust into her pussy from behind, taking the very breath from her lungs and starting her orgasm all over again.

Chapter Eight

Sam groaned through his clenched jaw as he thrust his throbbing cock into her pussy. Kaycee's hot, slick walls gripped at him, sucked him deeper, and he thought he'd die from the pleasure. Looking down, he gripped her hips and helped move her knees to the edge of the seat. She bent forward, her hands gripping the back of the couch, her breasts in Tyler's face.

Lifting his hands, his brother cupped her breasts then took one into his mouth. Kaycee whimpered and her pussy rippled along his cock, and he felt the vibrations clear to his balls.

With a growl of pure satisfaction, he pulled almost out, then thrust back in slowly, sighing as her walls sucked at him, pulling him deeper.

"Oh, God," he groaned, then did it again, this time thrusting harder, pushing her against Tyler's face.

Kaycee screamed, thrusting her hips back to meet him halfway, giving as much as she was taking. And God knew she was taking a lot. He and his brother weren't small by any stretch of the imagination, and on top of that, they could be incredibly demanding...insatiable. Especially, it seemed, where she was concerned.

He couldn't get enough of her and had proved it the previous night when he'd fucked her three times until they both finally collapsed from exhaustion.

Using his fingers, he spread the cheeks of her ass, admiring the tight, pink rosebud entrance to her tight ass. God, he wanted to take her there, show her how good it could be, but she wasn't ready. She needed preparation.

Unable to resist the enticement, he pressed his thumb into the opening, sliding it deep. She groaned, jerking her hips back for more. Her acceptance, her sultry whimpers and deep moans sent Sam over the edge. With a growl, he pounded into her. Keeping his thumb deep in her ass, he fucked her pussy hard, shoving into her repeatedly.

Tyler slid his fingers between her legs and stroked her clit. Her pussy shuddered and Sam grunted, trying to hold himself back, keep himself from spilling his seed before they could ring a third orgasm out of her. She screamed, her body tensing, her pussy walls spasming around him. His balls drew up tight and he shouted, thrusting one final time to empty himself into her hungry channel.

He held himself still, letting her walls suck the last of his seed into her body before gently removing his thumb from her quivering ass. With a sigh, he placed a kiss on the back of her shoulder and she sagged forward, dropping her head into Tyler's neck.

"Have we scared you off, baby?" Tyler asked and Sam tensed, waiting to hear what she would say.

She grinned, then rose slightly, or at least as much as she could with Sam still embedded in her pussy. Sam watched as she cupped Tyler's face, kissing him softly. She was so beautiful with her face flushed, sweat dotting her brow, the cheeks of her ass curved against his pelvis. He felt himself getting hard again and pressed into her, making her sigh against Tyler's mouth.

"Does that answer your question?" she whispered.

"Hell yeah," Tyler growled, his lips lifting into a grin. "Feel this," he whispered as he guided her hand to cup his hard cock. She didn't tense, or flinch like some women had done in the past when realizing they wanted to go again. She cupped him, stroked him, and Sam felt the walls of her pussy getting wetter.

"Damn," Sam growled and gripped her hips, holding her steady as he slowly slid in and out, pushing deeper with each thrust of his hips.

"Fuck Tyler, Kaycee," Sam murmured in her ear as he pulled out of her hot body.

Grabbing her elbow, he helped her to turn and face him, her back to Tyler, her hips straddling Tyler's cock. She frowned in question, until Tyler gripped her hips and thrust his cock into her. Beautiful green eyes widened in surprise, then drooped in pleasure as Tyler slowly fucked her.

Sam kept his eyes on her face, on the beautiful, passionate expression clouding her eyes. She was gorgeous and all theirs. Tyler had been right. She was the one. She belonged to them.

Feathering his palms up her chest, he cupped her breasts, letting his thumbs brush across her nipples. She moaned and threw her head back, her hips working over Tyler's. Sam leaned down and licked at a perky, extended nipple, and she shivered in his arms, her flesh blushing the most adorable shade of pink from head to toe.

"I like watching you," he whispered as his hands massaged her firm mounds.

She sighed in response, her eyes closing in pleasure. Her hands reached out to grip his cock and he had to clench his jaw to keep from shouting. Her fingers felt incredible as they stroked his length, clenching and unclenching around his shaft.

"I want to taste you, Sam," she whimpered and every part of him trembled.

He knew the second her lips closed around his cock, he'd explode, but he couldn't deny her anything. Stepping up onto the edge of the cushions of the couch, he braced one hand against the wall behind her, gripping her hair with the other and pulling her face toward his cock.

Her lips opened, engulfing him in her hot mouth. He groaned, grinding his teeth to keep from coming. God, she felt good, her mouth so warm and soft, he wanted to jerk his hips forward and bury his cock at the back of her throat, hold her steady while he shot her mouth full of cum.

Sam groaned, holding onto his control by a thin thread as she stroked his length with her tongue and teeth. Her cheeks sank in as she sucked him hard, making him gasp as pleasure raced through his veins, making his balls draw up tight.

"That's it, darlin'," he ground out. "Suck it."

As Tyler thrust into her from below them with a faster tempo, her licking at Sam's cock became hungrier, more desperate. She was close, so close. And damn it, so was he.

"Oh, yeah, baby," Tyler shouted and thrust upward hard, sending her headlong into another orgasm.

Her fingers dug into the flesh of his thighs as her pussy ground against Tyler. Her breasts bounced with her movements, her skin flushed a darker pink with her exertion and pleasure as she erupted around them.

She whimpered, a vibration whispering along his shaft, and he thrust forward, the head of his cock hitting the back of her throat. She swallowed and the movement rippled along his length, taking the last of his control. With a loud shout, he emptied his semen into her throat, his hands gripping her hair, holding her steady as he erupted within the tight confines of her throat.

He sighed and pulled his cock from her mouth with a pop, then gently stroked her hair as she drooped forward, laying her head against his thigh.

"Oh, God," she groaned. "Bath. Please, one of you, get me to a warm bath."

* * *

Tyler strolled into the kitchen early the next morning, the smell of eggs and bacon filling his nose as he inhaled. Sam stood at the stove, stirring the eggs. He glanced up and gave him a sideways grin. "Kaycee still sleeping?" he asked.

"Oh, yeah," Tyler said. "She was exhausted."

"Me, too. Many more nights like that and I'll be useless on the ranch."

Tyler chuckled, silently agreeing. Damn, she was hot. Shifting his jeans over his hardening cock, he dropped onto one of the island stools. Sam narrowed his gaze.

"Give her a break, Tyler. I think we fucked her enough last night. At least give her a few hours to recoup before you go attacking her again."

Tyler snorted. "Like you don't want to go fuck her again right now."

"That's beside the point. She has to be sore. I don't have a clue when it was we finally got to sleep."

"Around three, I think," Tyler murmured as he pulled the financial section from the paper and opened it.

The house phone rang and Sam reached over to grab it from the charger next to the fridge.

"Hello," Sam replied. "What?" He dropped the receiver beneath his chin and nodded toward Tyler. "They think they might have another victim."

Tyler perked up and waited impatiently for Sam to get off the phone. When he finally hung up, he snapped. "What happened?"

Sam sighed. "One of the nurses from U.T. hospital was killed last night. They found her body this morning. She was murdered in the same manner as the others, but she didn't look like Kaycee."

"He strayed from his norm. Do you think he was after information?"

"The only info he could have gotten were her records. It has your name, but the address is the FBI building. Not the ranch."

Tyler's nerves tingled. This wasn't good. "It wouldn't be that hard to track me down, Sam. Especially if they know what they're doing. You'd be amazed what you can find out on the Net." He pointed outside, toward the barn. "The hands know not to say anything, right? About Kaycee being here?"

Sam nodded. "I talked to them, but you can never be one-hundred percent sure."

Tyler rubbed at his eyes. He could see it now. All it would take was one paparazzi finding out her location for there to be swarms of them here. She was too damn high profile. That's why they couldn't take her into town. Why they had to keep her here, sequestered like a prisoner. So far, they'd been lucky. He just hoped their luck held out.

* * *

Kaycee felt something warm blow across her nose and she winced, opening her eyes to see what it was. She laid on the edge of the bed, nose to nose with Duke, his hot breath panting across her cheeks. Duke whimpered softly, then licked her nose with his wet tongue.

"Ah, Duke." She giggled, reaching up to wipe away the drool. With a smile, she ruffled the fur behind his ears. "Good morning to you, too, handsome."

Rolling to her back, she glanced around the room, noticing the empty bed and the sunlight streaming through the open curtains and across the hardwood floors. Outside the window, she could see the ranch hands on their horses in the distance. Even from here, she could tell it was Sam giving them their orders for the day.

He sat so tall in the saddle, so strong. One fist rested on his thigh as the other gripped the reins, holding his black horse steady as he pranced beneath him. Over the last few days, she'd noticed small things about the men's personalities and the way they carried themselves that made telling them apart easier. Turning her gaze back to Duke, who sat by her bed expectantly, she smiled.

"Tyler in his office?"

The dog tilted his head and barked as though to say yes. She giggled and sat up to grab her robe draped across the foot of the massive bed. With a smile, she slid her arms through the soft sleeves, then reached to the floor to grab her slippers. Those two were going to spoil her -- putting her robe on the bed, making sure her slippers were within reach.

Maybe a ménage relationship wasn't so bad after all. Although she didn't have a clue how she would explain it. But would she really have to? She frowned as an idea came to mind. They were identical. If only one of them went... She shook her head. No. That wouldn't be right to the other.

She could always quit modeling. She'd been thinking about it anyway before this happened. It had become boring, monotonous. She wasn't having fun anymore, so to her that meant it was time to get out.

With a sigh, she stared at the dog. "I'm getting ahead of myself, aren't I, Duke?" He tilted his head, studying her with those big brown eyes. "I mean, they haven't said they love me. And I don't even know if I love them. Just because the sex is…well, the sex is incredible, that doesn't mean we have a future together. Does it?"

Duke licked his chops, then yawned as though he found the whole thing boring. She snorted. "You were loads of help, Duke. Thanks."

The dog barked and she chuckled, wondering why on Earth she hadn't gotten a dog herself. She loved them, but her schedule was just too crazy. With a pat to his head, she stood and padded her way through the quiet house to Tyler's office at the far end.

He sat at his desk, his gaze intently studying the computer screen, his brow creased in a frown. He wore a navy blue suede shirt opened over a lighter blue T-shirt and she couldn't help but admire how well the color suited him.

She rapped her knuckles against the door softly, getting his attention. "Am I bothering you?"

He smiled, making the worry lines across his forehead disappear. "Of course not, baby."

The endearment made her heart jump, but the heated look in his eyes as they took in her robe, made it pound.

"Did you get enough sleep?"

"Yeah," she replied with a nod as she strolled forward. Her gaze flicked to the computer and he quickly closed the Internet window. "Doing research?" she asked, suddenly suspicious. He certainly closed that computer screen awfully fast.

"Sort of." He turned to shuffle papers, keeping his gaze down, and Kaycee scowled.

"Tyler Warren. Are you keeping something from me?" she demanded, her anger rising.

With a sigh, he turned his high-back leather chair to face her. "Of course not, baby."

She scowled. "You sound like a broken record." Tyler's lips twitched in amusement, which only served to make her angrier. "Please don't do this. Whatever it is that man is doing affects me, so therefore I should be kept in the loop."

He nodded. "I agree with you...except on this."

"Damn it, Tyler," she growled.

Spinning on her heel, she started to walk away from him. The sound of the chair scraping across the floor as Tyler stood sounded in her ears just before he grabbed her elbow, stopping her. With a gentle jerk, he turned her to face him. She was so close to him she had to crane her neck to look in his eyes -- eyes that watched her with worry, concern, and desire. She swallowed, so shocked the only thing she could think about was kissing him.

"We think he killed another woman," he said softly and she stopped breathing, fear gripping her chest. "I was looking at the pictures."

"They took pictures?" she gasped.

"They always do, baby. It's evidence. They took pictures of you, too. Don't you remember?"

She frowned, struggling to remember the first few hours after she'd arrived at the hospital. "I think so," she sighed with a shake of her head, quick flashes of camera bulbs going off in her mind. "Maybe."

"I'm not trying to keep things from you, I promise. I just don't want you to see that." He swallowed and glanced down at her chest. He reached out with one finger and traced the lace edging of her robe. "You don't want to see that, Kaycee. And I hope to God we can keep you from ending up the same way."

"Did she look like me?" she whispered, trying not to think about the gentle brush of his finger against her skin.

"Not like the others."

"Why did he stray from the norm? Didn't he always kill women that looked like me?"

Tyler nodded and feathered the back of his fingers along her jaw. "We think he killed her for information. She was a nurse at the hospital."

With a gasp, she stepped back and stared at him. Fear tightened her stomach and made her ill. She wanted to believe she was strong, but the idea of having to face that man again sent terror racing through her veins.

Tyler gripped her shoulders, bending slightly so he could look her in the eye. "Don't worry, Kaycee. We'll be fine."

"There was nothing in those records that could trace me to here?" she demanded.

"No," Tyler replied, but for some reason Kaycee had the distinct impression he'd just lied to her.

"Sam said he would be heading to town shortly for supplies and a few groceries. Is there anything you need?"

She shook her head in slight confusion. The sudden change in topic threw her for a second. "Uhmm, I'm not sure. I'll check."

"Write down what you need and I'll take the list to Sam."

She frowned. "You don't even want me leaving the house? It's just to the barn."

Tyler's lips twitched in amusement, making her stomach flutter. "Not dressed like that."

She glanced down at her thin robe and smiled. "Oh, yeah...I guess that would be a bad idea, huh?"

"Well," Tyler drawled. "Only if you don't want Sam attacking you in the barn."

She raised an eyebrow. "You mean like you did?"

He cleared his throat, making her grin. "I wasn't myself that day."

Kaycee snorted. "Apparently, neither was I."

With a sexy chuckle, Tyler moved close to her and tilted her chin up with the crook of his finger. Her whole body tensed in sexual need. God, she was easy where they were concerned.

"Go make me a list, then I'll cook you some breakfast." His gaze dropped and his lips morphed into a sexy grin that sent tingles down her spine and straight to her womb. "Take pity on me, Kay, and put some clothes on. Otherwise, it will be me attacking you instead of Sam." Turning her, he gave her butt a hard pat, sending little sparks of pleasure to her core. "Scoot."

With a frown, she reached around and rubbed at her smarting hip. "Did you just spank me?"

"Yep," he drawled. "And if you keep standing there, you'll get another."

Grumbling about arrogant cowboys, she went to the bedroom to make her list and change clothes. She should put tampons on the list just to freak him out. She grinned, imagining a red-faced Sam as he searched the isle for whatever tampons she put on the list.

She giggled, rummaging through the massive walk-in closet for jeans and a sweater. With a frown, she stopped and looked around at the empty room. Why did Tyler and Sam stay upstairs if they had this huge bedroom down here? Her gaze moved to the built-in set of lingerie drawers as her mind remembered the huge three person tub and shower in the bathroom, the three sinks, the king-sized bed. Was this the master suite they planned to share with their wife?

Her gut clenched as she imagined them with someone else. Another woman sleeping in the bed she'd shared with them last night. She swallowed down a lump of jealousy, slammed the closet door, and threw her clothes on the bed. Just the thought of them touching another woman made her angry.

"You all right?" Sam's voice called from the doorway and she jumped in surprise.

Spinning around, she stared into Sam's concerned gaze. He leaned against the doorframe, his jacket thrown over his arm, his Stetson in his hand. "I heard the door slam. Tyler piss you off again?"

His voice held a hint of amusement and she scrunched her nose at him. "No. I just…" She let out a sigh. Hell, she couldn't even think of an appropriate lie.

She finally shrugged. "Just letting off a little bored steam."

Sam snickered. "Okay. Did Tyler tell you I'm heading to town?"

"Yeah." She nodded. "I'm working on a list for you."

"Okay. I'll be in the kitchen."

With a wink, he left the room, leaving her staring after him like a love-struck fool.

Oh my God. Am I falling in love with them?

Chapter Nine

With pursed lips, Kaycee studied herself in the bathroom mirror and tried to comb her fingers through the thick, wet mass of tangles surrounding her head. Instead of joining the men in the kitchen, she'd quickly made a small list for Sam, then decided to take a shower. She needed time to think anyway.

Last night had been wild. The fact that she was having sex with two men didn't shock her. The fact that it felt right did. What exactly did that mean? She frowned into the mirror.

Am I reading too much into it? Was it just the heat of the moment and any two men would have brought me such pleasure?

She snorted and reached for the comb. She had limited experience with men. That she could admit. There had been men who'd kissed her and made her weak in the knees. There had also been men who'd made her shudder in disgust.

Her gaze widened. *Men who made her shudder.* She gripped the counter as her mind went back to the night she was kidnapped. Her attacker's eyes seemed familiar -- the look in them as he watched her slide to the ground. She knew she'd seen that look before. But from who?

"You look like you're thinking about something awfully hard."

Kaycee shifted her gaze and stared through the reflection of the mirror at Tyler. He leaned against the bathroom doorframe, his arms crossed over his chest, his heated stare glued to her open robe, which exposed her breasts.

"Sam back yet?" she asked, subconsciously closing the open lapels of her satin robe.

"No. He'll be gone for a while. He had a lot of stops to make."

She nodded, trying to control the sudden wave of heat settling in her core.

"It's just you and me," he said, his lips spreading into a sensual grin.

She smiled back. "So what's on the agenda for this afternoon?"

"A surprise for you."

"A surprise? What kind of surprise?"

Her heart raced as she watched his gaze go from mildly sensual to full-blown blazing.

"Something that will help get you ready."

He pushed away from the doorframe and for the first time, she noticed something in his hand. Her stomach flipped. It was long, but not thick -- probably about the width of her first and second fingers. It flared at the base with a small handle for gripping. Her ass clenched at the thought of him sliding that deep inside her.

He set the plug on the counter, then met her gaze in the mirror, his hands on her shoulders.

She swallowed a lump of trepidation. "I'm supposed to walk around all day with that in my ass?" she asked.

"Trust me," he whispered, and goose bumps skimmed along her flesh.

Reaching around her chest, his fingers gripped the collar of her robe and pulled it back and off her shoulders, letting it fall slowly and sensually down her arms. The warm, humid air of the bathroom hit her naked flesh and she shivered.

"You're beautiful," he murmured as his lips gently brushed along the column of her neck.

Tilting her head to the side, she welcomed his kisses. His lips were warm and soft against her skin. Her stomach began to tighten in need as warmth gushed to her pussy. Warm, strong palms reached around to cup her breasts and she dropped her head back against his chest, sighing toward the ceiling.

"So damn pretty," he whispered. "Look at yourself, Kaycee."

Opening her eyes, she hardly recognized the woman leaning against Tyler. Her breasts were full and erect, her skin flushed, her nipples hard, her eyes glazed over with passion. As she watched, Tyler feathered one hand down her stomach. It slipped between her legs to cup her shaved pussy and she bit down on her lip.

"So smooth," he murmured as his fingers separated her labia and slid through the juices coating her mound. "And so wet." His teeth scraped across her shoulder making her gasp softly. "I like it when you're wet."

Removing his hand, he held her gaze in the mirror as he lifted his fingers and sucked them into his mouth. She sighed, mesmerized by the hungry heat in his stare.

"Mmm, delicious," he whispered, then reached for the plug.

Her heart raced in her chest. She'd never done anything like this, but part of her hungered for it, ached for it. He pushed the plug between her legs from behind, sliding it through the juices that coated her pussy, wetting the tip. Blood pounded through her veins as Tyler teased the opening of her anus. He pressed forward slightly and she gasped, inhaling a quick shot of air.

He pulled back, then pressed forward again, this time pushing past the tight ring of resistance to settle deep inside her channel. The biting pain burned at first, then a burn of a different nature took over. She swallowed, watching Tyler through the mirror as his hands roamed over her hips. Every part of her was on fire. God, he'd done it so fast. Made her so crazy for him -- his lips, his hands, his cock.

"Tyler," she whimpered.

He kissed the side of her neck, his hot breath scorching her sensitive skin. "Need a little relief, baby?" he purred and she nodded.

"Like that a little more than you thought you would?" he coaxed as his fingers pinched and pulled at her sensitive nipples.

Swallowing her sudden desire to scream at him to fuck her, she gripped the counter with shaky fingers. "Yes," she said, her voice raw with need.

"What do you want me to do, Kaycee? It's your choice. Lick your pussy till you come?" She sighed, closing her eyes against the erotic image of him doing just that. "Or would you rather I get you off with my hand?"

His hand slid lower, teasing the edge of her pussy, just below her lower stomach. Her hips jerked, desperate for the touch he denied her. Juices coated the insides of her thighs as she struggled to keep her composure, struggled to keep from begging.

"Or would you rather I fill you up with my cock?"

His teeth bit down on her earlobe and she shuddered. "That," she gasped. "Please, Tyler."

Her face burned in embarrassment that he could get her to this point. That he could actually make her beg for it.

"Go get on your hands and knees on the bed."

With a gentle shove, he directed her toward the bedroom. She gripped the doorframe as she passed, unsure her shaky legs would carry her that far. Tyler must have understood, because he came up behind her and lifted her in his arms. With a surprised squeal, she wrapped her arms around his neck and held on as he strolled quickly to the massive king-sized bed and set her carefully on the edge.

Her position pushed the plug deeper and she shifted, moving to her hands and knees as he'd directed. Over her shoulder, she watched as he stripped out of his clothes, his gaze heated and staring straight at her ass.

"I think I like you with that plug in there," he murmured as he shoved his jeans down his hips, allowing his thick, hard cock to spring free.

She sighed hungrily at his size and her pussy clenched in need, forcing more cream from her core. God, how had she been able to take all of him? He was huge.

Narrowing his gaze sensually, he placed one knee on the bed. "God, that's so hot, baby."

His deep voice oozed over her like warm oil, so sensual and sexy. His palm feathered across her hip, then down between the cheeks of her ass, his fingers tugging gently at the handle of the plug. She gasped, pressing back as he slowly pulled the plug out. He stopped, his lips lifting in a purely male, predatory grin before he thrust it back in, wringing a deep groan from her as her womb tightened in response to the pleasure-pain building along every nerve in her body.

He leaned down and nipped at her neck. "Imagine how it will feel when it's my cock buried to the hilt in your ass." Her pussy and ass clenched, pulling the plug deeper.

Bending, he put his head between her legs. His hot breath teased her opening, making her pant with want quickly eating her alive.

"Such a pretty pussy," he whispered, then slid his tongue through her juices.

She whimpered, spreading her legs wider to give him better access. God, she wanted more -- needed more before she exploded. With a moan, Tyler thrust his tongue into her dripping vagina and she gasped, shoving her hips back for more.

"This plug in your ass will make your pussy even tighter."

Tyler stood straight behind her, settling the head of his bulging cock at her entrance. Her fingers gripped the covers, her body tensed, waiting for that initial, delicious invasion of his shaft.

He pushed forward slowly, a long, low groan leaving his chest as he slid deep. The juices coating her walls eased his entrance into her tight passage. She gasped, whimpering as her walls tightened and clenched around his thick girth, sucking him deeper. Pulling almost out, he then pushed back, a hiss filling the room as he buried himself to the hilt.

Kaycee could hardly breathe as the duel invasion of both Tyler and the plug raced through her with alarming speed. She felt full, consumed, overwhelmed as he gently began to move. Filling her over and over, thrusting, and demanding a response from her oversensitized body.

With an animalistic growl of her own, she shoved back against him, meeting every plunge of his cock, taking all he could give her.

"God, Tyler," she cried, shocked at the pleasure racing up her back as her anal muscles contracted around the plug.

Sharp, tingling currents of immense pleasure captured her whole body and her limbs tensed, her womb contracted. Tyler groaned as his thrusts increased in tempo, pounding into her so hard she thought she'd fall over. Bracing her hands against the mattress, she shoved back.

"Damn, Kaycee," he shouted. "Come for me, baby."

She whimpered as every part of her tingled in a mixture of pleasure and pain. She leaned down slightly: her nipples brushed against the mattress, making her gasp. Her pussy clenched, creamed, then exploded. She screamed, tears gathering in her eyes at the intense feeling of rapture that wouldn't end. Tyler kept thrusting, shifting slightly so he could pinch her clit, and the pleasure began again, throwing her into a pit of blinding pleasure.

"Oh, God. Yes!" she screamed.

"That's it, baby," he cooed, then thrust one final time, shouting her name as he spurted his seed deep into her rippling channel.

* * *

Sam looked at the list and chuckled. *Tampons.* She didn't need those. He knew she'd had a period while in the hospital. She had another two weeks before she would have another one. But he grabbed a box anyway and with a grin, he tossed it into the buggy.

If she'd done it to freak him out, she'd wasted her time. It didn't bother him. If he were honest, he'd admit he loved the idea of buying her tampons for the rest of her life. Double-checking his list to make sure he had everything, he began to make his way to the front of the store.

On his way to the register, *Sports Illustrated* caught his eye. Actually, it was the girl on the cover.

Picking it up, he studied the woman. With widening eyes, he realized it was Kaycee. She was on her knees, her arms curled over the top of her head. Her hair was damp and her eyes sparkled with mischief as she gave the camera a half smile. The purple bikini left little to the imagination, showing off her cleavage, long luscious legs spotted with sand, and a flat, firm stomach. He frowned, looking closer. Was that a belly button ring?

She wasn't wearing one now.

His cock twitched at the thought of tugging at it with his teeth. Belly button rings were so sexy, and hers was a killer. But with the gorgeous cover came doubt. My God. She was on the cover of *Sports Illustrated*. Could he and his brother really convince her to throw caution to the wind and accept a ménage relationship? What if the press found out? What kind of embarrassment would that cause her? What would be the legal ramifications of two husbands? What would it do to her career?

He sighed heavily and studied those beautiful eyes. Eyes he could drown in. Damn. He was lost…a goner…screwed…he was in love with her and it was high time he started really fighting for her. To hell with the press and the legal ramifications. He and Tyler had already worked all that out anyway in the event they'd be lucky enough to find someone. Legally, she would be his wife, but emotionally she'd be bound to both of them.

With a wicked grin, he tossed the magazine into the buggy along with the groceries. Looked like a stop by his friend's tattoo parlor was in order. She needed another belly button ring. A sexy one. Sam's grin widened.

* * *

Strolling through the house, Sam set two bags on the table, then went in search of Kaycee. He found her in the bedroom, huddled under the covers against Tyler, her hair spread across the pillow in a soft mass of curls.

Sam smiled and bent down to gently brush the bangs from her brow.

He tugged playfully at her earlobe. "Wake up, sleepy head."

With an adorable kitten-like stretch, she turned to smile up at him, her eyes droopy from sleep. "What time is it?" she asked.

"Around three," he replied, then tossed the magazine onto her lap. "Check out what I found at the store."

With a frown, she picked up the magazine, then bolted upright, making Tyler's eyes widen in surprise.

"Oh, my God! I made the cover?" she exclaimed.

"You didn't know?" Sam asked in confusion.

"No. We never do until right before the magazine comes out. But I guess my agent couldn't get a hold of me to let me know."

"Let you know what?" Tyler asked as he, too, sat up and glanced down at the magazine. "Damn, is that you?" He grabbed it and pulled it closer so he could see it better. His eyes narrowed slightly before glancing back toward Kaycee. "Where's the belly button ring?"

"The what?" she asked with a slight giggle.

Tyler pointed toward her stomach. "This."

"Oh. I took it out for the shoot I had with Jean Claude the night I was kidnapped." She shrugged. "It's probably still back at my house."

"Damn," Tyler grumbled, making Kaycee giggle.

"I take it you like belly button rings?"

"Hell, yeah," Sam replied with a grin as he reached into his pocket and pulled out a black box.

Kaycee's eyes widened slightly as she stared up at him with uncertainty. "What is that?"

"Something I picked up this afternoon. A friend of mine has an upscale tattoo parlor on the edge of town. Thought you might like it. I know I will."

She took the box from his fingers and opened it. Her full lips dropped open on a silent 'oh' as she stared at the belly button ring. A half carat diamond glittered just above a one carat diamond -- both of them connected by a small gold chain.

"Sam, please tell me these aren't real," she whispered as her fingers gently nudged at the diamonds, watching as the light caught and enhanced the blue color within the stone.

"Why would I do that?" he teased.

She shook her head and started to hand it back to him. "Sam, I can't --"

"Yes, you can," Sam replied, keeping his voice low, but firm. "That's just as much for me and Tyler as it is for you." His lips twitched. "And I can't wait to see you in it."

Her gaze narrowed. "The two of you are going to be the death of me, you know that right?"

Tyler snorted. "Death by sex. Hell of a way to go."

* * *

Stopping his car, he climbed out and glanced around at the small town of Dumas. It hadn't been too difficult to track him down. Tyler's name was all over the Internet along with his twin brother, Sam. The two of them were quite the local heroes, having solved many missing person's cases for the FBI.

Interesting that they would bring Kaycee here. She always had a soft spot for small towns and ranches. He needed a few more supplies, then he could head off to the ranch. His cock twitched in anticipation of getting his hands on his elusive target. Fucking that nurse last night hadn't helped, not like the others. Closing his eyes, he remembered her screams, her pleas for him to stop the pain, to just kill her.

"Beg me," he growled down at her as he pounded his cock into her pussy. She was dry, so he pulled out and coated his cock with her blood, then entered her again, sighing as her tight walls gripped his shaft. "Beg me, damn you, Kaycee. Beg me to fuck you."

"Please," she sobbed, her voice weak. "Please, just kill me."

"Oh, I'll kill you, bitch," he growled. "As soon as I've had my fill."

He smiled, remembering the taste of her blood, the feel of it as he smoothed it over her skin. In his mind, he imagined it was Kaycee. Imagined he finally had the cold bitch in his hands.

His hunger for Kaycee was growing and growing fast. He would get her this time, or die trying.

Chapter Ten

Kaycee stood at the huge picture windows gazing out at the cold rain drizzling down across the ranch. A fire burned in the hearth behind her, but a chill worked its way up her spine anyway. She had a terrible feeling -- one that wouldn't go away. She still believed there was something about those pictures and it drove her crazy trying to remember. With a sigh of irritation, she turned away from the darkening sky and headed to the kitchen to see if she could help Sam with dinner.

Wonderful smells of garlic and basil filled her nose as she got closer; she inhaled deeply and smiled. "Sam, that smells wonderful. What is it?"

He smiled softly, his gaze studying her like he knew something bothered her. "Lasagna."

"Do you need any help?"

"You can take care of the salad. All the stuff is in the fridge. Add whatever you want."

She grinned coyly, watching desire flare in Sam's eyes like a flickering flame. "How about a little piece of you?"

He chuckled. "Oh, you'll get a piece of me, all right. After dinner."

A shiver of lust ran down her back as she opened the stainless steel refrigerator to get the lettuce and tomatoes. Feeling very mischievous, she whispered as she brushed past Sam, "I'm wearing the ring and the butt plug."

Sam stilled, then turned to her with narrowed eyes full of lust. She almost laughed, but instead bit down on her lip and turned her attention to the salad.

"Where did you get a plug?" he asked.

She shrugged. "Tyler."

Out of the corner of her eye, she watched Sam swallow. "It's going to be a long dinner."

Tyler strolled in, a bottle of red wine in one hand, three crystal glasses in the other; he set the glasses on the table with the plates and napkins. Standing straight, he watched the two of them for what seemed like endless seconds. One hand rested on the back of the wooden chair, the other on his hip. Dark blue Levis hugged trim, firm hips, and Kaycee's flesh heated as she remembered what lay hidden behind the zipper.

"What?" she asked.

Tyler shrugged. "Nothing. It just looks good, that's all."

"What does?"

"Seeing you help Sam in the kitchen."

She smiled softly and dropped pieces of torn lettuce into the wooden salad bowl. "It's surprising that a model can do such things, huh?" she teased.

Tyler chuckled. "I have a feeling you can do most anything you want to, Kaycee."

"Even some things I didn't even know I wanted to do." Her face heated with embarrassment and she dropped her gaze back to the salad.

In her peripheral vision, she saw Tyler strolling her way. Her breath caught as he placed a whisper-soft kiss on her cheek. Blood ran molten hot through her veins as her anal muscles contracted around the plug she had in her ass. It never failed to amaze her just how fast they could turn her on.

"How did you become a model? Was it something you always wanted to do?" Sam asked, pulling her thoughts away from the reaction her body had to Tyler's kiss.

"Actually, no. I had never thought about being a model. When I was in college, this man came up to me in a coffee shop and handed me his business card. He was a photographer for a well-known modeling agency in New York. At first, I just shrugged it off, but my best friend researched him on the Web, then insisted I go to the interview. They signed me that day."

Sam snorted. "Women who have been trying to break into the business for years probably hate the sight of you."

Kaycee grinned. "Yeah, I've run into a few of those over my career. At first the modeling was a part-time thing, just to pay the bills, then I started getting more and more assignments and I had to drop out of college. I was careful with my money and I could go back to college now if I wanted to, but I'm not sure what I want to do anymore."

"Are you not going to stay in modeling?" Tyler asked.

Kaycee detected a hint of anxiety, but didn't question him on it. "I don't know." She shrugged. "I was getting tired.

Bored. It wasn't fun anymore and I was actually thinking about trying to get out of my contract early."

"How much time do you have left on it?" Sam asked.

"One more year with the agency, but two with Revlon. The Revlon one I would finish out. Those shoots are actually fun. But I would like to step back from the other stuff. Do something else." She grinned and set the tomato on the cutting board. "Like maybe become a chef." With a wink, she lifted the knife and pressed down through the middle of the tomato.

"What do you think about ranching?" Sam asked, and she turned to stare at him in surprise.

"I don't know," she began slowly. Was Sam asking if she would like to stay here with them? The idea certainly had appeal, but wasn't it too early to talk about that? What was she thinking? Hell, she'd been having sex with both of them. Wasn't that moving fast too? "I haven't had much of a chance to do anything since I've been here. There are these two, really overprotective cowboys who keep me sequestered inside the house."

"That'll change in time," Sam drawled with a wink, sending a tingle of heat down her spine.

Taking a deep breath, Kaycee moved back to the fridge to look for other salad ingredients. "What about you guys? The FBI can't pay that much. How did you get this ranch?" She glanced around the door. "If that's not too personal."

"You can ask us anything you want, Kay," Tyler said, pulling out a kitchen chair and sitting down.

"The ranch was our grandfather's," Sam began. "Our dad didn't want it. He hates the country, so he gave it to me and Tyler. It was already a money maker, but we made some improvements, changed a few things here and there, and now it grosses over a half million a year."

Kaycee coughed. "How much?"

"A half mil," Sam replied, his lips twitching. "Tyler and I make a good team. I'm good with managing the ranch."

"And I'm good with the money and investments," Tyler added. "The two of us together are probably worth over ten million."

Kaycee stood staring at them in shock. After modeling, she was only worth about six million, so it was amazing they could turn this ranch and a few investments into that kind of money. "Maybe I should have you take a look at my portfolio."

Tyler smiled. "Anytime."

"Are your parents still alive?" she asked, handing the salad bowl to Tyler to place in the center of the table while Sam pulled the garlic bread and lasagna from the oven.

"Yeah, they live in Amarillo," Tyler said. "They would like you."

"You think so?" she asked, suddenly very concerned about what their family would think of her.

"Our mother would adore you," Sam said with a grin as he placed a basket of bread next to the salad. "Our dad would probably drop to his knees and bow in awe at the fact we brought home a supermodel."

Kaycee laughed as she sat in the chair next to Tyler, trying to picture that image and also trying to find a comfortable position with the plug up her ass. "So your family knows that you guys share?"

"Oh yeah," Tyler said as he scooped salad onto her plate. "Our mother knew first. Well, actually I think she figured it out when I was looking moon-eyed at one of Sam's girlfriends. We had a long talk and I told her how I feel what Sam feels and vice versa. She was a bit shocked at first, but she was the one who eventually helped me work through everything. She was also the one who suggested that there was one woman out there made for us -- one woman who would love us equally."

She couldn't turn her gaze from Tyler's searching one. He believed that woman was her. He'd told her as much, but she wasn't as convinced yet. Yes, she was attracted to both of them, but was it love and was that love real?

Finally, tearing her gaze away, she took the basket Sam passed to her and placed a garlic roll on her plate. A soft, sad whine came from somewhere off the kitchen and all three looked to the laundry room with a frown.

"What is that?" she asked.

"Sounds like Duke," Sam murmured.

Kaycee immediately stood and rushed to the laundry room door, Sam on her heels. She could hear Tyler's chuckle from behind her. "I guarantee it's Duchess getting even."

Coming to a stop, Kaycee stood and stared down at the doggie door, laughter lodging in her throat. Duke was outside the door, his nose pressed to the clear plastic.

Duchess sat with her back against the door from the inside, effectively blocking Duke's entrance.

"Duchess," Kaycee scolded. "Let him in."

The cat looked up at her with narrowed golden eyes then blinked as though not the least bit concerned. Again Duke whined, his nose nudging at the door. "He's a heck of a lot nicer to you than I would be," Kaycee grumbled. "I'm surprised he doesn't just barrel in and knock you over."

Sam laughed and she turned to smile at him over her shoulder. He stood just inside the door, one hand on his hip, the other on the doorframe and a wave of heat swam through her veins. "Come on, your high and mighty. Step away from the door," Sam ordered in a firm yet amused voice.

To Kaycee's astonishment, the cat meowed, then ever so slowly, stood and stretched, making sure to take her time as she arched her back. Her tail stood straight up as she stretched out her legs, sticking her ass right at the door as though to moon the dog.

Pressing her lips together, she held in her laughter as the cat slowly strolled past them. Duke barreled in and with murderous intent took off after the cat, who was now running for her life toward the living room. A book fell to the floor, probably the one Tyler had been reading earlier, just ahead of Duchess's hiss of anger toward Duke, who barked in response.

Belly laughing, Kaycee dropped back into her chair. "Those two are hilarious."

"I told you," Tyler said with a smile. "Entertainment."

Sam sat back in his seat as well and reached for the bottle of wine. "But when they think you're not looking, they're sleeping side by side in front of the fireplace."

"How long have you had them?" she asked, lifting the glass of wine Sam had just poured to her lips.

With a sigh, she let the sweet taste fill her mouth and warm her blood. One or both of them had great taste in wine. It was fabulous.

"Duke and the cat are both about four years old," Tyler replied. His eyes narrowed slightly as he studied her face. "How well can you hold your alcohol?"

"Depends on what it is," she answered with a shrug. "Wine, I can tolerate better than hard liquor. Why?"

"It would probably be best if you don't get too drunk. If we have to move fast for any reason, you'll need all your wits about you."

She stared at the glass and slowly set it back down on the table. "Oh, you're right. You know, sometimes I can almost forget why I'm here."

And truthfully she could. She had fun with them -- felt comfortable with them and every day that passed only drew her closer to her two gorgeous cowboys.

"Have the two of you ever brought any other women here to protect?" she asked, curious.

Sam shook his head. "No. We're profilers, missing person's investigators. We made an exception for you, so you should feel special." He winked, making her blood run molten hot.

"Oh, I do," she purred.

"If you think you feel special now, just wait until later," Tyler drawled.

Kaycee smiled, but inside, her stomach fluttered nervously and her burning anal muscles tightened around the plug. The earlier sensation of both Tyler and the plug inside her still had her senses reeling and the plug wasn't anywhere near as big as Sam. Could she really do it? And would they be upset if she couldn't? Slowly chewing her bite of lasagna, she studied them, remembered what she knew of them.

Both had said they wouldn't rush her and they hadn't. They'd been gentle, except when she'd begged them not to be and hadn't in any way made her feel uncomfortable. And whenever she thought about sex with both of them her body would heat with desire. It was a fantasy many women thought about, but few explored. Now she had the opportunity, but to Sam and Tyler it was more than just a fantasy. They hadn't said they loved her, hadn't even proclaimed to be developing feelings for her, but she did know they saw this as more than just playtime.

God, she wished she knew what the hell she was doing.

* * *

Sitting on the hotel room bed, he sifted through the pictures he'd brought of Kaycee. One caught his eyes and he smiled, remembering the day he'd taken it.

"Smile, Kaycee," he yelled, and she turned from staring at the ocean to smile back at him softly.

The soft wind blew her hair back, exposing her sun-kissed face, and he snapped the picture. Squinting, she raised her hand to block the bright Key West sunlight. Her white swimsuit cover rode up her thighs and he caught a quick glance of her long, shapely legs before coming back to her face.

Kaycee had a fuller figure than most models, but that had been part of her appeal. She carried it well and it showed. His gaze studied hers as she watched the coastline. Sadness filled her eyes. Sadness she tried to hide but couldn't. She wasn't enjoying herself anymore and although she never acted as anything other than professional, when not in front of the camera, it showed.

"Aren't they supposed to be here by now?" she asked, concern tugging at the corner of her eyes.

"Yes," he answered, then glanced around the roped off beach that had been picked for the photo shoot. He pointed to a group of cameramen and equipment coming through the back door of the hotel. "There they come. Claire," he yelled over the seagulls flying by. "Fix her hair and makeup, we should be starting soon."

"Yes, sir," Claire said, and waved Kaycee over to the tent that had been set up for just that purpose.

After making sure the equipment was being set up properly, he headed to the break tent and stepped inside the cool interior. Kaycee sat in a canvas director's chair, facing the large, lighted mirror. Claire worked with her hair, giving it a damp, just from the water appearance. "Five minutes, Kaycee."

She gave him a slight smile of acknowledgement.

"You look beautiful," he whispered.

And she did. So beautiful it made him ache to look at her and not be able to touch her. She'd kept her distance, letting him know without words they were friends only. Every time he came too close, she would back away as though loath for him to touch her.

He'd tried once -- kissed her at a party. Unfortunately, he'd become a little too overzealous and scared her off. She'd been careful to keep her distance ever since, but that night she'd made it perfectly clear she didn't think of him in that way.

Anger rolled through him as he remembered that night, remembered how badly he'd wanted her. He'd show Kaycee just how much they were meant for each other. After tonight, she'd be his and only his.

Standing, he strolled to the window and stared out at the rain pouring down. He couldn't do anything tonight. But he knew where the Warren ranch was located and it would only be a matter of time.

* * *

Kaycee stared at her reflection in the bathroom mirror, admiring the yellow lace panties and bra. With the tip of her finger, she brushed at the belly button ring and watched as the bathroom lights made the diamonds sparkle brilliantly. She still couldn't believe what Sam had done. He had to have paid a small fortune for this.

Smoothing her hand down lower across her lightly tanned flesh, she took a deep breath for nerves and decided to take the bull by the horns. She'd been thinking about it all day. Sex with both of them. It was high time she made her thoughts a reality.

With a quirk of her lips, she left the bathroom and headed to the living room. Tyler stood at the window watching the rain while Sam stoked the fire, making the orange flames lick higher.

"Think this rain will let up by tomorrow?" Tyler asked, a frown creasing his brow.

"According to the weather channel, it will. Should let up sometime tonight," Sam replied.

Standing straight, he stopped, dead still as he stared at her. "Holy shit," he said, and sighed.

Tyler turned to look as well and his eyes widened.

"Surprise," Kaycee said, her lips spreading into a shy smile.

She knew she was pretty, but she'd never been the seducer. All the other men she'd been with had seduced her. Not once had she taken the initiative and been the one to act first. Until now.

The look in both their eyes made her blood pound through her veins. Her stomach knotted as she wondered what to do next. Sam held out his hand, beckoning her to him, his gaze alight with burning desire, nearly setting her skin aflame.

Taking another deep breath for courage, she stepped forward and grasped his fingers. He tugged her to him as one arm circled around her lower back. Smoldering blue eyes held a promise of passion and her heart skipped a beat.

"God, you look incredible," he whispered just before his lips touched hers in a deeply tender and erotic kiss.

His lips brushed back and forth, teasing hers as he gently sipped and licked at her lower lip. She sighed, opening her mouth, silently welcoming the invasion of his skilled tongue as it delved inside to explore. Her knees grew weak and she lifted her arms to wrap around his neck, holding on tight.

Tyler moved in behind her, pressing his bare chest to her back. *He'd removed his shirt?* The heat of his flesh seeped into hers, warming her, burning her as his hands reached up to flatten against her stomach between her and Sam. Warm lips touched the side of her neck and she moaned into Sam's mouth -- his unbelievably hot, delectable mouth.

Sam's hands wandered lower, over the rise of her hips, then around to the side to tug at the lace of her panties, pulling them lower. Tyler joined his hands as well, helping Sam to push her underwear down her legs to pool at the floor. Cream leaked from her pussy, coating the inside of her thighs. Her whole body felt overly sensitive -- responsive to even the slightest touch.

"My turn," Tyler murmured as he gripped her chin, tugging her away from Sam.

Moving behind her, Sam allowed Tyler to take his place and begin his own assault on her senses. His kiss was so different than his brother's but at the same time, so much the same. He tasted of Italian spices and wine, smelled of tomatoes and musk, even a hint of wood smoke clung to his skin, making her flesh tingle.

Sam's fingers worked the back of her bra loose and he slid his hands around to cup her breasts. Tyler tugged the lace down her arms, letting it fall to the floor, forgotten. Arching her back a little she pushed her breasts more fully into Sam's hands. Tyler broke the kiss and she bent her head to watch as he lowered his and suckled the breasts Sam held up in invitation. With a groan, she closed her eyes, burying her hands in Tyler's hair to tug him closer. His mouth felt so good on her sensitive nipple, so hot as he licked and bit, suckled and teased.

She felt the loss of Sam's heat as he moved away and circled behind Tyler. She watched, mesmerized as Sam removed his clothes, exposing inch after inch of hard, tanned, perfectly formed flesh. She swallowed at the sight of his engorged shaft, the tip glistening with precum. God, they were both so damn big. Was she out of her mind?

For a fleeting second, trepidation ran through her veins, but the second Tyler captured her lips with his again, she forgot it and instead let herself be pleasured by them, consumed by them. It felt right. Safe.

"Move her to the couch," Sam ordered, and Kaycee shivered at the raw hunger she could hear in his deep tone.

Tyler helped her to move to the couch, but instead of laying her on the cushions, he pressed her back over the armrest. With a gasp of surprise, she found herself lying in a strange position with the back of her shoulders flat against the cushions and her ass still on the armrest, her pussy bared. Tyler shifted to the side and removed the rest of his clothes while Sam stood between her legs.

"This is hot," he purred, then flicked at the belly button ring with his finger. "You, with nothing on but this."

Leaning down, he licked his tongue over it, then tugged at the ring with his teeth. She whimpered, panting now for air. Any air.

With a mischievous smile, he spread her thighs; she gasped as the cool air of the room hit her hot, wet mound. Sam dragged a finger through the thick juices coating her labia, and her hips bucked.

"This is perfect," Sam murmured as he lowered his head and blew against her pussy. She groaned and her body tensed, wanting much more.

With a slow draw of his tongue, he licked up her slit, making her shudder in need. A need so strong she felt as though she were drowning. "Oh, God," she groaned as more cream leaked from her core.

"Hmmm," Sam purred as he gently tugged at the plug in her ass. "You still have the plug in."

Kaycee gasped as pure sensation raced from her anal passage clear to her womb. In gentle shallow thrusts, he fucked her ass with the toy as his mouth returned to her pussy, feasting on her.

Fighting for air, Kaycee clenched at the cushions, wanting to grind her pussy against his face, wanting him to stop teasing and give her what she really wanted.

"Sam," Tyler whispered, and Kaycee opened her eyes to see him hand Sam a larger plug.

She held her breath as Sam met her gaze and pulled the smaller plug from her ass. Placing the cold tip at her entrance, he waited for her to relax, then gently pressed the tip past the tight ring of resistance. She swallowed, closing her eyes against the burning, intensifying pain as it morphed into extreme pleasure.

"This one is closer to our size, Kaycee," Tyler whispered in her ear as he leaned down next to her. "But if we hurt you, just say so."

She shook her head and took a deep breath, trying to force herself to relax.

"Push out a little, baby," Sam ordered and she did, which allowed the toy to slide even deeper.

Her eyes flew open as she felt the muscles give and then clench, sending pleasure racing up her back.

"That's it, baby," Sam whispered, then leaned down to lick at the juices pouring from her vagina. "Just a little more." Pressing it forward, he buried it as far as it would go.

She whimpered, her hips grinding helplessly against Sam's mouth. The pleasure-pain had almost sent her careening over the edge. All it would take was one flick of his tongue on her clit to send her soaring. Tyler's tongue licked over her distended nipples and she arched her back, fighting the intense pleasure wanting to take her over.

"Oh, God," she panted, desperate now for some kind of relief, but he held back, prolonging her torture.

"I can't wait to get my cock buried inside you," Tyler whispered against her mouth and she parted her lips in silent invitation for his tongue to slip inside. "Fucking you just as Sam fucks your ass."

Tyler's tongue fucked her mouth, showing her exactly what he intended to do to her while Sam's fucked her pussy. Her hips undulated wildly until Sam put a hand on her lower stomach, holding her still. She cried out then, desperate for her release.

"Damn it, Sam. Please," she pleaded.

Sam pulled away and she sobbed, her hips lifting from the couch, blindly seeking out his touch again. The two of them traded places again, but this time, Tyler gripped her hands and tugged her to a sitting position on the armrest. She gasped as the movement sent the plug even deeper, sending a sharp bite of pleasure-pain to her core.

Tyler picked her up in his arms, carried her to the bedroom, and laid her on the mattress. She stared in unabashed hunger as he moved between her legs, and dipped his head to feast on her saturated pussy. Kaycee screamed, lifting her hips from the bed to grind her pussy against his face, forcing his tongue deeper into her channel.

Sam moved to Tyler's old position and licked at her nipples, his teeth gently biting down, and she squealed in surprise. "Like that, baby?" Sam asked, his lips spread into a devilish grin.

"I'm going to shatter if one of you doesn't do something," she panted

"How about if we both do something? Would you like that, Kaycee?" Sam asked.

She nodded, almost begging now. "Yes."

Tyler moved to his back and Sam helped her to climb over his hips. Before either of them could stop her, she slid down his length, taking all of him balls deep. She stilled, gasping for air as his thick girth plus that of the plug overwhelmed her.

"Son of a bitch," Tyler growled. "She's so fucking tight."

"Are you okay, Kaycee?" Sam asked from behind her, his voice full of concern.

She took two deep breaths, letting her body become accustomed to the dual invasion, then nodded her head. "Yeah. I think I should have went a little slower."

Tyler pressed upward, seating himself even deeper and she closed her eyes on a groan. Her nails dug into Tyler's chest, leaving half moons on his skin.

"Oh, my God," she sighed as the pain began to subside and pleasure took its place. Intense pleasure she never imagined existed, and something she wasn't so sure she could handle.

"Ride me at your own pace, baby," Tyler whispered as his hands rested at her waist, strictly holding her up, but not guiding her.

With slow movements, she began to experiment. With each stroke of her pussy down Tyler's shaft, she became bolder, more confident.

"Oh, fuck, yeah," Tyler murmured and his fingers flexed at her waist, digging painfully into her skin.

The pain only spurred her on, intensified her pleasure as she rode Tyler's thick cock, taking all of him inside her. Sam moved back behind her and tugged at the plug. She stilled, panting, waiting for what she knew he was about to do.

"Come down here, baby," Tyler murmured and put his hand at the back of her neck, pulling her down so that he could kiss her.

His tongue thrust past her lips to invade her mouth and she moaned, giving herself over to him completely. She felt Sam nudge at the tight entrance to her ass and she pressed back almost forcing his cock inside her hole. Sam gripped her hips, holding her still.

"Damn, darlin. You're gonna kill me if you keep that up."

Slowly, Sam pushed forward and like with the toy, she pressed out, allowing him to sink inside her tight ass. He growled as he thrust hard, burying himself almost balls deep. At first the sensation took her breath and she broke the kiss to drop her head to Tyler's chest. She could hear his heart pounding just as fast as her own, could hear his ragged breathing as he held himself back.

"Oh, God. I can't breathe," she whispered as Sam pulled back, then pressed in even deeper.

"Are we hurting you?" Tyler asked, and her heart burst at their compassion and gentleness. How could any woman walk away from this? How could they have walked away from them?

"No," she cried, fighting back the tears. She never imagined she'd feel anything like this and she didn't want it to end. "Just fuck me, please. Make me come."

Sam began to move first, then Tyler, each of them thrusting in perfect unison. Kaycee could only lie there and take it. Take both of them as they kept building that pleasure, stroking her channels until she thought she'd die from sheer ecstasy.

Their rhythm began to build, to quicken, and her body responded. Every nerve ending pulsed, every muscle trembled as her release neared, threatening to wring the very life from her. Everything blurred. Her body erupted into a ball of pleasure as her womb contracted, sending her pussy and ass into spasms.

"Damn," Sam growled as he thrust deeper, taking the very breath from her lungs. "God, Kaycee, the way your ass is squeezing my cock feels so good."

Kaycee couldn't answer. Her whole body shook as her orgasm gained in strength, sending her screaming even higher. She cried, sobbed as she fought to stay conscious, fought to keep from losing her mind.

"Stay with us, baby," Tyler cooed, although she could hear the strain in his voice.

"It feels so good," she cried, then screamed as Tyler reached between them and pinched her clit, sending her over the edge into another release. "Don't stop. Oh, God, please don't stop."

"Fuck," Sam groaned as he pressed forward, faster, harder, pounding into her over and over. With one final thrust he emptied his seed into her ass.

Kaycee could feel every throb of his cock as he came and her anal muscles tightened around him, milking him further. Tyler gave one hard thrust upward as he, too, found his release with a shout, filling her with his hot cum.

Closing her eyes, Kaycee gave up the fight and allowed herself to slip into blissful darkness.

Tyler felt her go limp and brushed her hair from her face with a shaky hand. "I think she passed out," he whispered.

With a sigh, Sam leaned down and placed a kiss on the top of her head. "Can't say as I blame her."

"Me, either," Tyler said with a sigh of his own. *Damn, that had been amazing. But would she feel the same? Or would this scare her off?* "The others weren't like this, Sam."

"I know," he whispered then pulled partway out.

Kaycee moaned and they both stilled, watching her face. Her eyes remained closed and the frown slowly faded from her forehead. Slowly, Sam pulled the rest of the way out.

"I'm going to go get something to clean her up with."

Tyler nodded and wrapped his arms around Kaycee's shoulders and held her tight. She snuggled closer, sighing as she molded her body to his. Rolling his eyes, he sighed toward the ceiling. His damn cock was getting hard again. Her hips wiggled against his shaft and he swallowed, feeling it swell even more as her tight walls gripped and rippled along his length.

"Tyler," she murmured and he smiled, thrusting his hips up slightly, watching her lips part on a sigh.

God, the woman was a dream. A fucking perfect dream. Sam strolled into the room and helped Tyler lift her off his cock and roll her to her back. Spreading her thighs, Sam pressed the warm cloth to her pussy and she sighed, bucking her hips off the bed.

Sam's eyes widened with surprise and lust. "Damn, if she keeps that up, I'll have to fuck her again."

"You sound like that would be a bad thing," Tyler teased.

With a grin, he traced his finger around her distended, rosy nipple. She was beautiful with her skin flushed pink, her hair mussed and tangled, her thighs wet with her come and theirs. She'd responded to them perfectly. Even now in her sleep, he could see the awakening desire in the response of her body as Sam gently cleaned her pussy.

Her eyes opened and she stared at them with confusion and a hint of smoldering desire. "What are you doing?"

"Cleaning you up," Sam replied.

Sliding the rag lower, he cleaned between the cheeks of her ass. She sighed and closed her eyes. "Are you sure that's what you're doing?"

Tyler chuckled at the husky quality to her voice.

"Oh, I'm sure there's lots of other things we *could* be doing," Sam purred, then bent down to lick his tongue up her slit. "God, I love your taste."

Kaycee smiled. "I can't believe after what we just did, that I could want you again."

With a moan, Sam suckled her pussy in earnest, the sounds of his pleasure muffled against her mound as he licked at the cream pouring from her vagina.

"Tyler," she murmured and buried her fingers in his hair, tugging him down to her. "Kiss me."

With a smile, he covered her lips and did just that.

Chapter Eleven

Kaycee woke the next morning sore and unbelievably satisfied. She stretched along the sheets, enjoying her few minutes of solitude. She'd heard Sam and Tyler earlier when they'd gotten up and she'd started to join them, but Sam had pushed her back down under the covers with strict instructions for her to get more sleep.

She had to admit, they'd worn her out. But it was a good wore out. She was sore in places she didn't even knew existed, but she'd loved the feeling of total joy, total pleasure as they'd both fucked her. Taking two men was nothing like she had imagined and everything she'd hoped it would be.

She glanced at the bedside clock and noticed the late hour. It was past noon? Wow, she really must have been tired. Sitting up, she grabbed her robe from the foot of the bed and went in search of Tyler. She found him at the kitchen table, a stack of papers spread out before him. A pair of glasses perched on his nose and she frowned.

"I didn't know you wore glasses," she said, and Tyler raised his gaze to stare at her over the rims.

His lips spread into a welcoming smile, making her feel warm all over. Reaching up, he tugged them off. "Yeah, I wear them sometimes." He shrugged and grinned sheepishly.

"Usually only after I've gotten a headache from trying to go over this stuff without them."

She laughed and came further into the room. "Any coffee?"

"I made a pot just for you."

She smiled at him as she poured coffee into the mug he'd set in front of the pot. "Don't you like wearing your glasses?" She thought he looked quite good in them herself.

"It's not that I don't like wearing them. Most of the time, I just don't want to have to track them down. I can never remember where I last took them off."

"Maybe you should keep a spare or two."

He grinned and tapped at the glasses. "That's what these are."

With her cup in hand, she strolled back to the table and took his outstretched hand in hers. With a gentle tug, he pulled her down to place a soft kiss against her lips that made her flesh feel warm and tingly.

"How are you feeling this morning?" he asked, softly.

"Sore," she admitted as she stood straight again, trying to ignore the tingling warmth spreading up her arm at the feel of Tyler's fingers grasping hers. "But nice. No desire to run just yet, even if there wasn't a lunatic after me."

Tyler stood, taking the very breath from her lungs as he stared down at her, his eyes smoldering. "If Sam or I begin to overwhelm you, tell us."

She swallowed. "Why would you think you're overwhelming me?"

"Because right now, I'd like nothing more than to lay you back on this table and fuck the hell out of you."

"Oh," she replied, her eyes widening.

God, even her pussy clenched at his huskily spoken words. Raising her hand, she pressed her palm against his chest. The strong pulse she felt beneath her fingers made her feel safe, secure…empowered. Would this all-encompassing desire ever wear off? Would they always be able to turn her into a pile of mush by just looking at her?

"Take a shower with me," she whispered.

Tyler opened his mouth to say something but the phone rang, cutting him off. "Hold that thought."

With a sigh, Tyler strolled over to the phone and glanced at the caller ID. John Mills. He was a friend of theirs who owned the local Exxon station in town. Hitting the talk button, he brought the phone to his ear.

"Hey, John," Tyler said.

Kaycee strolled over, wrapped her arms around his waist from behind, and rested her cheek against his back. With a smile, he put his hands over hers thinking just how right that felt.

"Tyler? Or is it Sam? I can't ever fucking tell the two of you apart on the damn phone."

Tyler chuckled. "It's Tyler, idiot. What do you need?"

"Listen, something weird happened this morning and when the hell did you start dating a supermodel?"

His gut tensed. "Hang on a second, John."

Tyler placed the phone against his stomach. "Kaycee, baby. Would you do me a favor before you get in the shower?"

"What is it?" she asked as she loosened her arms from around his waist.

He turned to face her, wanting desperately to join her in the shower, but he knew John and he never called anything weird without a reason.

"In my office, there's a walkie-talkie. Would you call Sam and tell him I need him to come to the house?"

Her brow crinkled into a frown. "Is anything wrong?"

He shook his head. "No. It's about the gas we have delivered up here for the ranch. We keep a pump out by the barn."

She nodded, but her gaze narrowed suspiciously. "Sure."

"Hey." He grabbed her hand, and then tugged her back to him. Leaning down, he kissed her lips, swallowing her soft sigh. "Take your time in that shower," he whispered. "I'll join you shortly."

"What about Sam?" she asked. "We had time alone yesterday. Will he be upset with us?"

Tyler shook his head with a smile. "No, baby. We lay equal claim to you."

With a quick peck to her lips, he sent her to his office with a hard pat to her ass. She frowned at him over her shoulder, but he just smiled devilishly, watching her go.

He waited until she'd left the room, then put the phone back to his ear. "What happened, John?"

* * *

"Something wrong?" Sam asked as he strolled quickly into the kitchen and threw his denim jacket across the back of a chair. He found Tyler sitting at the table, his brow creased into a worried frown.

"Seems our friend may have found us."

"What?" Sam snapped, fear for Kaycee almost choking him.

"John called. He said some guy came by the station this morning asking about me."

Sam shrugged with a frown. "Lots of people have done that, Tyler."

Tyler scowled. "This wasn't someone looking for the ranch, Sam. He was asking about me and when he found out I had a twin brother, he started asking about you."

Sam frowned. "What kind of questions?"

"He claimed to be a reporter from New York and he'd heard that I was dating that supermodel on the cover of *Sports Illustrated.*"

"Shit!"

"My words exactly. I had to explain to John what was going on and threatened him with castration if he told anyone else."

Running a hand down his face, he dropped into one of the kitchen chairs. "Where's Kaycee?"

"In the shower."

Sam nodded. "Go by the station and get Simms. He's a good sketch artist." He glared toward his brother. "John got a good look at his face, right?"

"For the most part. Said a baseball cap covered up a lot of it, but he thinks he can describe him pretty well."

"Good. I'll stay here with Kaycee."

Tyler stood and grabbed the jacket Sam had discarded. "Might want to join her in the shower."

"Why? Is she expecting you?"

"Yep. But something tells me she won't mind if it's you instead." With a wicked grin, Tyler headed out the door.

"Make sure the alarm is set," Sam called.

With a quirk of his lips, he looked toward the bedroom. No better way to guard her than to be in the same room with her.

* * *

Kaycee stood in the shower, letting the warm water wash away her stress and sore muscles. She'd bet every dime she had, Tyler had been lying about that phone call. Why did they think they had to keep things from her, that she was some fragile wallflower who couldn't take it?

The shower door opened and she lifted her head to see Sam standing amidst the rising steam. Naked, he looked like some Norse god coming to claim his prize and every part of her quaked in desire.

"Tyler had to go to town. Mind if I join you instead?" His deep voice rumbled through the shower, making her insides churn with mounting lust.

"Maybe," she replied. Turning, she put her hand against the metal frame and blocked his way in. "Only on one condition."

"There's conditions?" he asked, his lips twitching in amusement. "And what might those be?"

"That you and Tyler don't lie to me, or try to protect me by keeping me in the dark."

"Have we been doing that?" he asked, his head tilting slightly to the side.

"Yes, and you know it."

He stepped forward, crowding her against the tile wall. "You're right," he said with a nod. "I promise you, from now on we'll tell you everything. But right now..." He grasped her wrists, holding them together over her head with one hand. The other he used to follow a drop of water as it worked a path down her side. "Right now I want to help you forget."

Her heart raced as she watched the gentle teasing in his gaze morph to hungry desire. He made her crazy when he looked at her like that -- like he wanted to eat her alive, devour her whole. Every nerve ending under her skin prickled as his work-roughened palm moved to smooth over her hip.

"And how do you plan to do that?" she asked, her voice husky and strained.

"Oh, I have lots of ideas." His lips spread into a purely predatory smile. "Would you like for me to tell you some of them?"

She nodded, unsure she could do much else.

"I could eat your pussy...right here against the shower wall."

She shivered from head to toe, imagining him doing just that. His hand moved to cup her pussy, and she sighed, spreading her legs wider to give him better access.

"My, my," he whispered. "You're wet, darlin'."

She smiled as she felt his long, thick shaft pressed against her thigh. "And you're hard."

"So I am," he chuckled. "You tend to do that to me."

"Are we safe, Sam?"

He nodded. "I always have ranch hands watching the house and the alarm is on. We're as safe as we can be. Just relax, Kaycee," he whispered as he drew his fingers along her wet slit. "Don't think about it. Think about me filling you with my cock instead."

Her breasts swelled and her legs trembled at his words. That was all she could think about. One or both of them filling her, making her come and scream with pleasure.

"You'll feel so good," he whispered, then dipped his head to circle her hard nipple with his tongue. "Your pussy will be so tight and hot, squeezing my cock like a glove you're so tight."

His teeth scraped across her areola and she gasped as tingling heat swept through her womb. "And your ass," he purred, sliding his finger back to circle the tight hole. "God your ass felt incredible. Do you have any idea what it felt like to have your ass squeeze my cock when you came?"

She shook her head, watching helplessly as he bit at the sensitive underside of her breasts.

"It felt like you were milking me, draining me."

She swallowed, wiggling and trying to move her pulsing mound closer to his hand. His lips blazed a trail up her chest to the side of her neck. Heat burst in her core and radiated outward, making her moan softly.

Moving his hand back to her pussy, he slid one finger inside and pressed upward, almost lifting her feet from the wet shower floor. "Sam," she gasped, almost desperate now for more.

"I love your pussy, darlin'," he purred. "Such a sweet, slick, hot, little pussy."

He added a second finger, slowly fucking her with gentle, shallow movements that had her knees bending in an attempt to force them deeper.

"Do you know what I want to do to this pussy?"

"What?" she sighed, undulating her hips along with his fingers.

"I want to fill it with my cock. Fill it full, Kaycee."

His voice dropped to a deeper tone, sending tingles up her spine. He moved his fingers in scissor-like movements, stretching her. She moaned, opening her eyes to stare into his as he watched her. They were such a deep shade of blue, so fathomless, and ablaze with passion. She'd never had a man look at her like that -- look at her with such hunger, tenderness, and desire. It shook her to her very soul.

"Sam," she begged, but he shook his head, continuing to tease her with his fingers.

Dropping his head, he brushed his lips across hers, sipping lightly at her mouth. Her lips parted, inviting him inside, and the second his tongue swept into her mouth, she groaned, arching her breasts against him and hungrily returning his kiss. Her fingers clenched above her and she struggled against his hold, but he held her still, held her tightly within the grasp of his hand, dominating her, controlling her, and the very idea almost had her careening off that edge.

Breaking the kiss, she panted against his lips. "Sam, please."

"Mmm," he purred. "Hungry are you, darlin?"

"Yes," she sighed, desperately sucking air into her lungs.

"Tell me what you want," he ordered sensually against her lips, his fingers driving her insane as they slowly fucked her pussy.

"I want you," she pleaded.

His lips twitched and she almost groaned in desperation. She was dying and the damn jerk was having fun tormenting her.

"You want me to what?"

"Damn you, Sam. If you don't fuck me right now, I'll…"

"You'll what?" he teased, adding a third finger to her dripping vagina.

"I'll die," she whispered. "Oh, God, Sam. I'll die."

Letting go of her wrists, he used both his hands to grip her hips and lift. Her legs wrapped around his waist and her fingers latched onto his strong shoulders, holding tight as he thrust his cock into her with one hard, deep, delicious shove.

Her head fell back, hitting the tile wall behind her. "Oh, God, yes!"

"Fuck." Sam groaned as he pulled out, then pressed back in, seating himself even deeper.

She was angled perfectly and with every thrust of his cock, his pelvis brushed against her clit, making her womb clench. Ripples of pleasure skimmed through her veins and she moaned, angling her hips to meet his thrusts.

"Sam," she whimpered. "Oh, God. I'm gonna come. I don't want to come yet."

Sam pulled back, holding himself still with just the head of his cock inside her channel. She groaned, her hips jerking in reflex to take him deeper. His lips covered hers, his tongue stroking along hers sensually, and her whole body trembled. Breaking the kiss, he smiled.

"Better?" he murmured.

Warm water continued to rain down on them, soothing her. The droplets glistened on Sam's skin and sparkled in his dark hair. His lips were wet, full, and she licked her tongue along his bottom lip, making him shudder in her arms.

"I like that," he whispered.

Slowly, he pressed his cock inside her again and she could feel her walls tightening around him. Her mouth dropped open on a silent cry as he pressed deep, grinding his pelvis against her sensitive clit.

"I like that, too," he purred.

It was as though he never stopped and she screamed as her release raced through her, shattering her into a million tiny pieces. Sam groaned as well and increased the power of his thrusts, pounding into her so deep and brutal she thought he might shove her through the tile. Tightening her grip on his shoulders, she took it, begging for more as she angled her hips to take him even deeper, even harder.

With a shout, Sam emptied his seed into her pussy. She ground her hips, wringing even more from him as his cock jerked and throbbed inside her.

"Son of a bitch," Sam growled as he gripped her hips, holding her steady. Panting, he dropped his forehead to hers. "My God, Kaycee," he whispered.

"My sentiments exactly," she whispered. "The two of you are going to wear me out."

Sam chuckled, his left palm stroking her lower hip. "All you ever have to do is say no."

She snorted. "Yeah, right. How could I ever tell the two of you no?"

"Ah," he teased, his lips spreading into a grin. "The words every man loves to hear."

Closing her eyes, she sighed and ran her fingers through his wet hair. "This is crazy."

"I know. But as crazy as it is, it just keeps getting better."

That it did.

* * *

He stood on the hillside, about a quarter mile from the ranch house watching through his binoculars as one of the twins, which he wasn't sure, fucked his Kaycee. He had the most powerful binoculars money could buy. It saw right through the window and straight into the open bathroom door, where their gray silhouettes could be seen through the fog covering the glass shower door.

Anger knotted his stomach and his fingers tightened their grips, turning his knuckles white. She was his, damn it. His. That man had no right touching her. No right at all.

Lowering the binoculars, he scowled toward the house in the distance. He had to find a way into that house. And when he did, that son of a bitch would forever regret touching his Kaycee.

Chapter Twelve

Kaycee pulled at her damp hair, twisting it on top of her head, then secured it with a clip. Sam stood in the bathroom doorway, buttoning his shirt and watching her with the oddest expression on his face -- like he wanted to say something, but wasn't sure how. Somehow Sam didn't strike her as insecure or hesitant, so to see that side of him shocked her.

"What?" she asked.

He shook his head. "Nothing."

With a smile, he walked over and placed a quick kiss on her temple. His gaze met hers in the reflection of the glass and she caught the hint of worry in his eyes.

"Do you remember you promised not to keep anything from me?" she whispered.

Sam sighed and wrapped his arms around her shoulders, holding her back tightly against his chest. Her stomach knotted in concern. "What is it, Sam?" she whispered.

"That phone call from earlier?" he began and she nodded. "That was a friend of ours, John. Someone came by his garage earlier claiming to be a reporter and wanted to know about you and Tyler."

"Me and Tyler?" she gasped. "How would a reporter…you don't think it was a reporter, do you?"

He shook his head and rested his chin against the top of her head. "No."

Fear invaded her heart. Had he found them? "Where did Tyler go?"

"He went to talk to John, to see if he could get a description and draw up a sketch."

"What if he follows Tyler back?"

"If he knows Tyler's name, then he knows where the ranch is. It's not that hard to find out that stuff, especially if you know what you're doing."

"He got Tyler's name from the nurse he killed, didn't he?"

"More than likely." Sam drew in a deep breath and buried his face in her neck. "Stay close to us, darlin'. Do what we say, when we say it, without question. All right?"

She swallowed with a nod and gripped his strong forearms with shaking fingers.

"Promise me, Kaycee."

"I promise."

"If anything were to happen to you…" He sighed, but before Kaycee could say anything the walkie-talkie he'd laid on the dresser in the bedroom beeped.

She followed him out of the bathroom and watched as he picked it up, hitting the talk button. "Yeah, Juan, what is it?"

"It's FedEx, Señor Warren. They're coming up the drive. Do you want me to stop them before they get to the house?"

He looked up at Kaycee. "The pictures are here." Clicking the talk button, he once again spoke to his Foreman. "Can you see the driver?"

"Sí. It's Josh."

"Thanks, Juan. I'll take care of it." He gave Kaycee a firm look. "Stay here."

Running to the closet, Kaycee grabbed a blue sweater and jeans, then followed Sam to the foyer to meet the delivery man, despite his order to stay put. Sam opened the door, letting in a blast of cool air and smiled at the tall, younger man in a blue and white uniform.

"Hey, Josh," Sam greeted. "What have you got for me today?"

"Afternoon, Mr. Warren. Got a package from Washington," Josh replied with a grin. He caught site of her standing behind Sam and his eyes widened slightly before he gripped the edge of his cap, tipping it slightly. "Hello."

Sam turned to glance at her over his shoulder. He scowled, then nodded ever so slightly toward the back of the house. She scrunched her nose and headed toward the kitchen to make coffee. She never got to finish the cup she had earlier.

Sam stomped in after her just as she had finished measuring out the coffee grounds. She hit the start button and turned to face him. He looked angry, and her suspicions were confirmed when he dropped the large envelope onto the table with a loud whack that made her jump.

"Kaycee. I told you to stay put. What if he'd recognized you and ran his mouth back in town? Do you have any idea how small this town is and how much people talk?"

His tone made her bristle and she reacted to his anger, with rising anger of her own. "No, I'm afraid I wouldn't since you keep me sequestered here like a prisoner." She slammed the coffee can down on the counter and sighed, angrier with herself than Sam. She hated it when she spoke without thinking. Plus Sam was right. She shouldn't have let the FedEx guy see her. "I'm sorry. I know why, I do --"

"Kaycee, I promise, this isn't going to last forever." Sam gripped her shoulders and turned her to face him, giving them a gentle squeeze. "But we have to play this smart."

She nodded and bit down on her lower lip. "I know. I'm just getting cabin fever."

"I know you are, darlin'. And I'm sorry I snapped at you."

Moving forward, he wrapped his arms around her and gave her a warm hug. She melted against him, sagging into his embrace like a contented puppy.

"I suppose I deserved it," she mumbled, and Sam's chest shook as he chuckled softly.

"No, you didn't." Taking a deep breath, he rubbed his palms up and down her back. "Are you ready to look at pictures?" he asked.

"Yeah."

He pulled her to the table and sat down next to her as she opened the envelope and dumped the numerous snapshots onto the counter. They were all of her. Various pictures taken over what looked like a couple of years. One caught her attention and she lifted it to study the picture more closely.

She stood at a wooden railing, the ocean rolling behind her, the wind whipping at her hair. It was taken in the Keys. She remembered the view. She'd posed in front of that same railing for the shoot. She also remembered who took it.

With a gasp, she began to pick through the others. Two of her in Paris, one in Rome, a few others from modeling shoots, and one from her birthday party. It was the one of her and her agent. Turning to Sam, she tossed the picture onto the table.

"I know what it was about these pictures I was trying to remember. They were all taken by the same person."

Sam frowned. "Are you sure?"

"Yes. I have copies of all these. He gave them to me."

"Who, Kaycee?" he asked as he sat forward slightly, his brow creasing into a scowl.

"Scott Ferguson. He works for the modeling agency and is at almost every shoot I do."

The front door opened and Tyler yelled from the entryway. "Sam?"

"Kitchen," Sam called back and they waited as Tyler's boots stomped across the hardwood floor.

He slowed when he saw Kaycee, then glanced to Sam. In his hand was a rolled up piece of paper.

"She knows," Sam said and Tyler nodded, his eyes narrowing slightly.

Moving to the table, he cupped the back of her neck and softly kissed her lips. "Hey, baby. Enjoy your shower?"

The corners of her lips quirked in amusement. "Immensely."

Tyler chuckled and sat down in the chair opposite her and Sam.

"It was in the shower she made me promise to keep her in the loop," Sam drawled. "It's damn hard to deny her anything when she's standing there all naked and wet."

"I bet," Tyler replied with a chuckle.

The coffee maker beeped, letting them know the coffee was done. Kaycee stood, shaking her head at the two of them. "The two of you are impossible."

"Yeah, but we're good." Tyler waved the piece of paper. "We have a face."

"We also have a name," Sam replied and Tyler's eyebrow rose.

"Care to share?"

"Wait," Kaycee said, strategically grasping three cups in her hands. She moved quickly to the table and set the cups down. Taking her seat, she held her hand out to Tyler. "Let me see the picture."

Tyler placed it in her hand and waited quietly while she studied it. Her eyes narrowed and her cheeks drained of all color as she stared at the face. A face she knew so well.

Oh, God.

"It's Scott," she whispered.

"Who?" Tyler asked.

"Scott Ferguson."

Tyler leaned forward, his brow creasing. "Is this the name you had?"

She nodded and handed the picture back to Tyler. "I recognized the pictures. I have the same set back home. I know who took them. It was Scott."

Tyler stood and grabbed another piece of paper from a kitchen drawer, then handed it to her. "Write everything down that you know about him, Kaycee. Name, address, phone number. I'll give all the info to Barreck."

She took the paper and pen with trembling fingers. Sam noticed and covered her hand with his. The understanding in his gaze made her heart melt. "I can't believe I know him. He tried to kiss me once." Sam's fingers tightened around hers and she glanced down at his hands. They were large and tanned -- work-roughened, his fingers thick. They were a man's hands, strong hands. But at the same time they could be so gentle. "I told him I didn't think of him that way. It was weird...the kiss. It was almost brutal. And the look in his eyes..." She gasped and turned to stare at Sam with wide eyes. "He had the same look in his eyes when he drugged me. He hated me because I turned him down."

"Probably, but more than likely, he was crazy before that. He would have to be to do some of the things he'd done to those women." Sam raised his gaze to Tyler's. "Did you give the info to the local police?"

He nodded.

"So he's here in town," Kaycee murmured as she stared at the paper, her mind working. "What if we use me as bait?"

"Hell no!" Sam snapped.

"Why not?" she snapped back.

Tyler sat back in his chair, a thoughtful expression creasing his brow.

"Tyler," Sam growled in warning.

"I'm just thinking it through, Sam."

"The answer's no. There's no thinking through anything."

"He wants me, right?" Kaycee reasoned. "What if we try to make him jealous?"

"Make him jealous?" Sam snorted. "Great idea. Let's get the lunatic all riled up so he has even more reason to want to cut you to pieces."

With a sigh, Kaycee waved her hand. "You know the overprotective thing was cute there for a while, now it's just getting on my nerves."

Sam leaned forward, a menacing scowl hardening his face. "Do I need to show you pictures of what that man has done to his victims?"

"I've seen it firsthand, remember?" she countered back.

"Enough!" Tyler snapped and both of them turned to look at him in surprise. "I actually think it's a good idea."

Sam stood, almost knocking his chair over backward in his anger. "Are you out of your damn mind?"

Tyler stood as well, his eyes narrowing dangerously toward his brother. "We can get some other agents in on this, Sam. If you'd stop being so damn hardheaded, you'd see this could work."

"Work how, Tyler? What are we supposed to do? Have sex with her in the hot tub on the deck? In plain view of our killer as well as every agent stationed around the house? I may be into a lot of things, but exhibitionism isn't one of them."

"Who said anything about having sex?" she asked in exasperation.

Sam dragged his hand down his face, while Tyler pursed his lips with a nod. "I didn't." He glared at Sam. "I think it was you."

"Fuck you," Sam growled, snarling his nose at him.

"Stop it!" she snapped. "God, the two of you are worse than kids. We don't have to have sex to make him jealous." The heat of a blush moved over her cheeks and she tried to hide behind her coffee cup as she lifted it to her lips. "Besides, I don't know about the two of you, but after sex with you guys, I can't think straight enough to defend myself."

Tyler's lips twitched in amusement. "I have to admit, I'm not sure I'd be able to either. I'm thinking that one of us, it certainly doesn't need to be both of us, should be out on the deck with Kaycee in some sort of romantic setting. A few kisses, maybe, then bring it inside. See if he follows."

"How are we going to know he's watching?" she asked, suddenly very nervous.

"I'd bet money he's watching now," Sam snarled.

Kaycee's gaze shot to the French doors leading off the eat-in kitchen, her heart jerking in fear. She scanned the grounds past the barn, but couldn't see anything.

With a sigh, Sam touched the top of her head. She glanced up at him questioningly. "Are you sure about this, Kaycee?"

She nodded. "I want this over."

Sam swallowed and a sad shadow fell over his blue eyes. Her first instinct was to wrap her arms around him, tell him she wanted to stay here with them. But as good as the sex was, she still didn't know. It had all happened so fast and the last thing she wanted to do was make a huge mistake.

Do something, Sam. Tell me you love me. Tell me you can't live without me. Make me believe this is more than just incredible sex.

"Call Bareck. Tell him to get here with some men," Sam said before leaving the room and forcing Kaycee to swallow back a lump the size of a baseball.

* * *

Kaycee sat downstairs in the movie room, staring blindly at the movie playing on the screen. Sam had spent most of the afternoon working in the barn, talking with the ranch hands. He was distancing himself again and she didn't know what to do to fix it. Had he taken her comment that she wanted it over to mean she wanted them over as well?

She didn't. Or at least she didn't think she did. If only they would tell her how they felt. She needed to know the love she felt growing inside her wasn't just one-sided, that they felt it as well.

Tyler dropped onto the couch next to her and glanced at the screen. "What are you watching?"

She shrugged, keeping her gaze toward the movie. "I don't know."

"Scared?"

"Confused."

Tyler nodded. "Want to talk about it?"

"Is this for real, Tyler?"

"What, baby?"

"Us."

"I'd like to think it is."

She turned to look at him, tears in her eyes. "I'm scared."

"Of what?"

"Of getting hurt. Of hurting you and Sam. Of finding out once all this is over and real life sticks its nose in that none of it was real."

"It's as real as we make it, Kaycee." His hand covered hers, warming her cold fingers. "I know one thing for certain. With you here, everything feels right. Whole. You complete me and Sam." He lifted her hand, kissing the back of her fingers. "When the three of us are together, it's like a perfect union. A perfect peace. I'm not about to give that up without a fight."

A tear slipped free and fell down her cheek. Tyler wiped it away with his thumb. "Don't over think it, baby. Love should be emotion driven, not logic driven. If you feel it, it's real and that's all that matters. If you feel it now, you'll feel it when real life returns."

She sniffed, her lower lip trembling. "I hope it's that simple."

With a slight smile, Tyler slipped his arms around her shoulders, hugging her to his side. She rested her cheek against his chest, enjoying the sound of his even breathing, the pounding of his heart, and the warmth of his flesh through his clothes. Closing her eyes, she let his embrace soothe her and her body relaxed a little more. She felt right in his arms just like she felt right in Sam's.

"I know it's that simple," he replied, his voice rumbling against her cheek, and she smiled.

Maybe he was right. Maybe she should stop over thinking it and just let her heart move her in the right direction.

* * *

"Sam?"

Kaycee's arms slid around his waist from behind, and Sam closed his eyes. God, if he lost her, whether to Scott or her own fears, he didn't know what he'd do. It tore him up inside to think about having to face this house without her in it. He put his hand over hers, entwining their fingers.

"Talk to me, Sam."

He sighed and tugged at her hands, making her move in front of him. Turning her so her back was against his chest, he slipped his arms around her waist and held her close. "Just stand here with me, darlin'."

Her tiny body sagged against his and he smiled, enjoying the feel of her in his arms.

"It's beautiful out here." She sighed.

Sam nodded. The full moon cast a soft grayish glow over the ranch, lighting the pastures and hillsides behind the barn. Was he out there? Was he watching them now?

She's mine, you dirty son of a bitch.

"Tyler and I had a nice talk today," she began.

"Yeah?" he murmured, placing a soft kiss against the side of her neck. A tremor skimmed just below her skin and he rubbed her upper arms, warming them. "Are you cold?"

"No."

She turned in his arms to face him, her eyes wide and uncertain. She placed her small hands against his chest and he reached up to grasp them within his. Her lips lifted into a teasing smile, making his heart skip a beat.

"Don't you want to know what we talked about?"

"Maybe," he teased, wrapping one arm around her lower back to pull her close. Her breasts brushed against his chest and even through their clothes he could feel the firm mounds and nipples tighten. "Maybe I'd rather kiss you instead."

"Really?"

"Yeah. Besides, Tyler already told me what you talked about."

She backed away slightly, her eyes narrowing. "He did?"

He nodded. "And I agree with him. Don't over think it."

"So basically," she began, eyeing him through her lashes, "I can never have secrets with you two."

He pursed his lips, glancing toward the night sky. He looked back down at her, his lips twitching in amusement and brushed a lock of hair from her cheek. "Tyler and I tell each other everything. We always have. It's not like we can hide anything from each other."

She laughed softly. "You have a point there, I suppose. Now didn't you say something about a kiss?"

"Did I?" he purred, lifting her chin with his finger.

"Yes, you did."

His mouth brushed across hers and her lips parted, sending her minty breath floating across his lips. Cupping her cheeks with his palms, he licked at her mouth, teasing her. Small hands dropped to grip the fabric of his shirt at his waist as he deepened the kiss, sliding his tongue inside to stroke hers.

She responded instantly, sighing into his mouth as he twirled his tongue around hers, coaxing her to play with him, to match his passion. Pulling away, he smiled at her parted lips, silently begging for another kiss. He kissed her forehead, letting his lips linger against her warm skin. Her arms wrapped around his waist and he held her tight as she laid her head against his chest.

"This is where you belong, darlin'," he whispered.

* * *

Scott stood on the hillside overlooking the house, staring through his binoculars at Kaycee wrapped in one of the Warren brother's arms. Anger seethed through him.

Damn bitch. Damn fucking bitch.

Lowering the binoculars, he scowled toward the house. He would move closer, wait until she was alone, then he'd strike. He'd looked closely at the house earlier and its security system. Should be easy to bypass. The hands might be a problem though. He'd avoided them earlier, but tonight there was a full moon. Good for him in some ways, bad in others. He'd be able to see the house, but that also meant the ranch hands would be able to see him.

Thinking, he devised his plan of attack.

* * *

"Since there's a full moon tonight, do you think he'll try something?" Kaycee asked as she loaded the last dish from their late dinner into the dishwasher and closed the door.

The hum of the motor filled the quiet room. It was too quiet. Everyone was tense, on edge. Especially her. Despite how brave she tried to be, her fears made her stomach tighten in knots. All day today, every time she'd closed her eyes, she'd remembered Miranda and all the things that sick jerk had done to her. She'd been cut everywhere, her bones broken, her spirit smothered and battered.

How had she missed this? How could she have considered that man a friend? She closed her eyes as memories from the night of her party came back to her.

"Happy birthday," Jordan cried as she pushed her way through the crowd and wrapped Kaycee in a comforting hug.

Pulling back, her friend's gaze skirted around the massive room decorated in silver and crystal, the champagne flowing freely, and the buffet fit for a queen. "Damn, Scott really outdid himself, didn't he?" Jordan said with a grin. "I think he has the hots for you, girlfriend."

Kaycee cringed. "No he doesn't. He does this for all the models."

Jordan rested her fists on her hips and stared at her in amusement. "Didn't I see you at Shara's party? It wasn't anything like this. Scott's not bad. I think you could do worse and he knows the industry. He would be a whole lot more understanding than that last loser who always bitched about you being away so much."

Looping her arm through Jordan's elbow, Kaycee pulled her along as they weaved their way through the crowd. "He's just not my type."

"Why? Because he's nice?"

Kaycee shuddered. "He's weird."

"He's quiet."

"Jordan, please," Kaycee pleaded. "I don't want to date anyone right now, okay?"

With a nod, Jordan put her hand over hers. "Fair enough. I'll let it go but reserve the right to hound you again at a later date."

"Deal," Kaycee said with a laugh. If nothing else, she could always count on Jordan to make her smile.

"Oh, my God. There he is," Jordan squealed, spotting the new young model her agency had signed that week. "If I'm not back within the hour, don't come looking for me." With a wink, she moved off to flirt with the models, leaving Kaycee by herself. She wasn't alone for long, though. Her agent, Charlotte, spotted her and waved.

"There you are. I've been looking for you everywhere," Charlotte said as she came to stand next to her. "I swear,

Scott outdid himself tonight. Not only with the party, but with the guest list. Did you know the reps for Victoria's Secret and Gap are here? We've got to get you to meet them."

Kaycee shook her head, holding her hand up for Charlotte to stop. "This is my birthday party, Charlotte. Give me a day at least to breathe, would ya?"

Charlotte frowned. "What's gotten into you lately? Don't you like modeling anymore?" Her eyes narrowed. "You don't, do you?"

"I just need a break. I'm tired."

"A break's easy enough. I'll set aside some time next month for you to go to the Caribbean or maybe Fiji. I'll send Scott with you."

Kaycee scowled. The last thing she wanted was Scott with her on vacation. "Charlotte!" she snapped.

Her agent stared at her with wide, innocent eyes. "What?"

Kaycee started to open her mouth and tell Charlotte where she could stick both Scott and her vacation plans when the subject of her tirade called her name. She turned to look at him and frowned. Scott always had that damn camera. Like her picture wasn't taken enough as it was.

"Come on, ladies. It's a birthday party, Kaycee. You should look happy." Lifting the camera, he smiled, making his green eyes crinkle at the corners. "Smile for me. Come on, Kaycee, just one picture with your agent."

With a sigh, Kaycee put her arm around Charlotte and they both smiled at the camera, pretending everything was wonderful, pretending her life wasn't spiraling, smothering. Scott's camera flashed and he lowered it, staring at Kaycee as though he were trying to read her mind, and she shivered.

Scott wasn't a bad guy, not really. He just wasn't her type. He didn't do anything for her physically. But then lately, what man had?

"Oh, there's the editor for Vogue. *I'll be right back." With those words, her agent was off like a dog after a bone. God, didn't the woman ever stop?*

"You okay, Kaycee?" Scott asked, and she turned to look at him. Really look at him.

His dark blond hair was neat, short, his eyes expressive, his lips full. He had a nice body -- muscular, but not overly large. He really was a good-looking man, but he just didn't make her tremble. There wasn't a spark between them. Truthfully, she'd begun to wonder if that so called 'spark' even existed.

"Are you not enjoying your party?" he asked, and she blinked, reminding herself to pay attention to what he was saying.

"I'm sorry," she said, with a slight shake of her head. "The party is wonderful. You've done an amazing job, Scott. Thank you."

His smile was beaming. "I'm glad you like it."

She breathed in a deep breath of hot, smoky air and turned to Scott with a pleading look. "Please tell me there's somewhere I can get some air. I feel like I'm suffocating."

"Sure. Come on. I'll take you to the rooftop deck."

She stared at his offered elbow and almost backed out. She hadn't wanted him to come along, but she didn't have the heart to tell him that. Despite all his weird flaws, she didn't want to be mean to him.

Putting her hand around his elbow, she let him lead her to a doorway at the far end of the room. Inside was a staircase leading to the roof. She stepped through the door and drew in a sharp breath as a cold, New York breeze took her breath. Shivering, she wrapped her arms around herself, warding off the chill. But despite the cold, the air felt like freedom and the view was utterly amazing.

"My God," she said as she strolled to the edge of the roof, her gaze taking in the nighttime view of Manhattan from fifty stories up. "This is beautiful."

"Had you not seen the view?" Scott asked in surprise. "There must be hundreds of windows in that room."

"I know," she said. "I just didn't have an opportunity to look, I guess. But even if I had, this is different. It's so open up here. I feel like I can see forever."

"You haven't been happy lately, have you?" he asked, and she turned to face him.

"Does it show that much?"

He shrugged, his lips lifting in a slight smile. "Maybe just to me. I'm worried about you."

She frowned. "I'm fine, Scott, really. I'm just tired -- tired of all the backstabbing, the long hours, the lack of privacy, the nonsense. I just want to be normal for a while."

Scott stepped closer and brushed the back of his fingers along her cheek. His touch was warm, soothing and for a split second, she wondered if maybe there was more to him than she initially thought. His face lowered, his lips covering hers in a kiss that started out gentle, but the instant she began to return the kiss, it changed. His hands gripped her shoulders, holding her roughly as his mouth slanted almost brutally across hers, forcing her lips against her teeth. The metallic taste of blood filled her mouth and she gasped, trying to pull away, but he held her tighter, not letting go.

Anger raced through her. Anger and revulsion. What was he doing? His tongue stabbed past her parted lips and she shivered in disgust. Turning her head to the side, she was finally able to break her mouth free.

Gulping in air, she stepped back, glaring at him from a few feet away. His gaze narrowed, his eyes glowing in hatred, and her breath caught. My God. Was he nuts? "What are you doing?" she gasped.

He lowered his lashes, covering the anger she'd seen simmering in his eyes. When he raised them back to her, they were empty, cold, and she took another tentative step back. He was giving her the creeps.

"I'm sorry," he murmured. "I just wanted to kiss you."

She wiped at her lips, frowning at the blood on the tips of her fingers. Turning them, she held them up so Scott could see. "You call that a kiss?"

"I guess I got a little carried away. It won't happen again, Kaycee, I promise."

Kaycee shook her head. "Scott. I'm sorry. I should have never led you on and let you kiss me. I was upset and not thinking clearly. You're a good friend, and I want to keep it that way, but I don't feel..."

"You don't feel that way about me."

His eyes darkened again, making her shudder. Fear snaked down her spine. She'd been alone with Scott numerous times, but not once had she felt fear. He was a little odd, but he'd never scared her. Now he did and she quickly glanced around for the door back to the party.

"I'm sorry, Scott," she whispered. "I should probably head back to the party."

He remained quiet, his eyes watching, calculating. Taking a deep, shuddering breath, she turned her back on him and headed back to the crowded floor below.

Strong hands wrapped around her waist from behind and she flinched, stiffening against the strong chest now molding against her back. She tried to pull away as a sudden wave of fear gripped her, but the arms tightened, holding her close.

"It's me, darlin', relax."

Sam.

She immediately sagged against him, her trembling fingers moving to cover the hands at her stomach.

"You okay?" he whispered in her ear and she nodded. "Are you sure?"

"Yeah. I was just remembering the night of my birthday party. When did he kill the first girl?"

"Over a year ago."

She frowned. "That was before my party. Before he kissed me. He was killing women even then?"

"It's going to be okay, Kaycee. You look exhausted. Why don't you try to get some sleep? I'm going to work out a few details with Tyler."

Turning in his arms, she stood on her tiptoes to place a kiss on his lips. He smiled, tapping the tip of her nose. "Sleep tight, darlin'."

"You'll wake me when you come to bed?"

He nodded and kissed her forehead.

"Good night," she said. "Don't be too long."

"We won't be. We'll be in the kitchen if you need us."

With another nod, she turned and headed into the bedroom, shutting the door behind her. Sam's gut tightened in real worry. Something was up; he could feel it in his bones. As he headed to the kitchen, he grabbed the walkie-talkie from the coffee table.

"Juan," he said into the mic.

A few seconds later, his foreman responded. "I'm here, señor."

"You and the hands watch the house closely. Let me know if you see anything at all."

"Sí, señor."

With a tired sigh, Sam set the walkie-talkie onto the kitchen table. Tyler was already there, loading their guns. "We need Barreck here," Sam growled. "Where the hell are they at?"

"It takes time to get here from Washington, Sam," Tyler tried to reason, but all Sam could do was scowl at him.

* * *

Scott slowly crept up behind the ranch foreman, careful to keep his steps as quiet as possible. Raising his knife, he took a deep breath and wrapped his arm around Juan. The man struggled, but Scott had been prepared, knew how to hold him to be most effective.

With his other hand, he quickly sliced a deep path across the man's neck. Blood squirted out onto his hand and arm as the man struggled for air, gurgling sounds coming from his throat as he attempted to speak.

With a smile of satisfaction, Scott watched his skin pale and the light fade from his eyes. A feeling of euphoria crept through him, heating his blood, making him want more. He wanted to see that same fear on Kaycee's face, wanted to hear her beg him to kill her. Then she would truly be his.

Chapter Thirteen

Kaycee opened her eyes to find a hand clasped over her mouth. Fear tightened her chest as she stared up into the face of Scott Ferguson. How the hell did he get in the house? Sam and Tyler. Oh, God, what did he do to them?

With a whimper, she tried to shove the hand away, but he kept it firmly over her mouth, pressing her lips back against her teeth. From the corner of her eye, she noticed the open French door and wanted to cry. So that's how he'd gotten in.

Breathing in, she caught the metallic scent of blood and almost gagged from the wretched smell. It covered his hand and arm and her heart lodged in her throat. Whose was it?

"You're mine now," he hissed. "I know just how to kill you and take my time doing it. You'll scream for me, Kaycee. Scream for me."

She shook her head, her fingers trying to pry loose the hand he had clamped over her mouth. Realizing it did no good, she opened her lips and bit down. Her teeth sank into his flesh and the warm taste of his blood filled her mouth, but still he wouldn't let go.

He growled low in his chest, his face scrunching into a furious scowl as he raised his arm, bringing it down in a wide arch. She didn't have a clue what was about to happen until she felt the stinging pain of steel shoved into the lower-right side of her stomach.

Her body tensed and she cried out behind his hand. With a cruel twist of the knife, he pulled the blade free, the jagged edges of the metal tearing her tender flesh as it was removed. Her fingers trembled as she tried to cover the wound. Pain raced through her with every movement of her body, no matter how small, and she struggled to stay conscious. Blood seeped from the wound, covering her fingers and flowing onto the bed.

"Stupid bitch," he hissed.

She sobbed behind his hand, tears blurring her vision. Reaching out blindly with one hand, she knocked over the lamp next to the bed, sending it shattering across the hardwood floor. Her captor froze, his eyes narrowing into tiny slits of hatred as he lowered his face to hers. "I suggest you be still, bitch. I would hate to have to kill your boyfriend in front of you. I guess you need a little reminder of what I can do." He put the bloody knife blade in front of her face and she held her breath, quietly sobbing behind his hand. "I think I need to weaken you so you don't get away again."

She braced herself for another stab of his knife. But nothing could prepare her for the piercing pain as the tip sliced down the top of her thigh from hip to knee.

* * *

"What the hell was that?" Sam snapped as he and Tyler both looked toward the bedroom at the sound of shattering glass.

Duke stood, growling toward the bedroom door. Tyler and Sam both jumped up from their chair and ran to the bedroom door. Turning the knob, Tyler's stomach dropped to the floor when he realized it was locked from the other side.

"Kaycee!" he shouted, pounding his palm against the wood. "Kaycee, open the door!"

He turned to stare wide-eyed at Sam. "The French doors."

Sam nodded and took off to the deck to enter her room from the outside. Standing back, Tyler kicked at the thick oak, breaking the lock and shoving the door open. What greeted him made his heart plummet to the floor. Blood covered the sheets, but Kaycee was nowhere in sight.

"Where the hell is she?" Sam snapped as he came through the French doors.

Tyler shook his head, his gaze searching the floor for something they could use to connect with her. At the foot of the bed was her sweater from earlier Sam grabbed it and moved to stand next to him. Tyler's heart pounded furiously in fear. He didn't even want to think about what that man was doing to her.

"Grab it, Tyler," Sam ordered.

Tyler rubbed his fingers across his lips. "If he's killing her, Sam…"

"We have to do this. We have to find her."

Nodding, Tyler shoved aside his fear and grabbed one end of the sweater. Closing his eyes, he tried to focus. Intense pain raced through his body and he doubled over, gasping for air. "Son of a bitch," he hissed, dizziness making his vision blur. "She's hurting, Sam. Hurting bad."

Sam shook his head. "I can't see anything. She's got her eyes closed."

"She's conscious, but barely."

"Come on, baby," Sam coaxed. "Open your eyes. Show me where you are."

* * *

Kaycee moaned, her position slung over his shoulder making the pain rip through her abdomen. Where were Tyler and Sam? Why hadn't they come for her yet? Tears streamed down her cheeks and into her hairline. She didn't know how much longer she could hold on. The cut in her thigh burned, the pain in her stomach made her nauseous.

She had no idea where Scott was taking her, where he would kill her. She knew he would. She didn't have the strength to fight him. At the moment, she hurt so bad, she wasn't sure she even wanted to. The only thing that put any fight in her at all was the thought of Sam and Tyler. Were they okay? Were they hurting like she was?

She sobbed as Scott let her slip off his shoulder, and she landed on her back with a squeal of agony. Even the pile of hay she landed on didn't help to absorb the jarring shock of pain. Her eyes flew open as she struggled to catch her breath and remain conscious.

"You son of a bitch," she groaned.

Scott loomed over her, but she shifted her gaze to stare at the beams of the barn above him. If Tyler and Sam were okay and trying to find her, they would see what she saw -- they would know where she was.

"Call me names all you want, sunshine. By the time I'm done with you, you'll beg me to take your life. To make your life mine."

Her blurry stare shifted back to his haughty contorted smile. "What? You think you'll make me yours by killing me? You're insane."

His smile morphed into an angry scowl just before his hand reared back. She braced herself for the slap. Lightning flashed behind her eyes and blood from her busted lip filled her mouth, making her gag.

"I'm going to show you just how insane I am, bitch."

* * *

Sam's eyes tried to focus on what Kaycee was seeing. Beams. "She's in the barn."

Letting go of the sweater, he broke the bond and sprinted out the back door, Tyler close behind him. Duke took off as well, barking as he ran across the yard. Why hadn't Juan seen him? Warned them about him? As he rounded a curve in the path, he spotted a body and stopped, staring in shock at Juan's dead form. Regret gripped his chest as he turned to stare at Tyler.

"I'm going to kill that son of a bitch," he growled.

"Not if I do it first."

Both of them took off again, heading in the direction of the barn, praying they made it in time.

* * *

Kaycee struggled to stay awake, to ignore the pain. In the distance she could hear Duke barking and she rolled slightly so she could see the main doors.

"Why here?" she gasped. "Why the barn?"

"So they'll find you," he replied.

Bending down, he ripped her shirt, exposing her bare breasts to his gaze. With a leer he brushed the sharp point of his knife across the top of her breasts, making her tense in fear.

"I want them to see what I'm going to do to you. How I'm going to make you mine."

Kaycee could hardly breathe as she braced herself for whatever torture he had planned while at the same time her heart sank. Where was Sam? Where was Tyler? Why weren't they saving her?

Duke burst through the main doors, growling and barking as he raced forward and leaped toward Scott. Scott raised his arms to shield himself as Duke shoved him to the barn floor.

"No, Duke!" Kaycee cried and reached out her hand.

If anything happened to that dog because of her, she would be miserable. Scott shifted, shoving the dog off him long enough to stand. Kaycee caught the glint of steel as he made a move to lunge toward the dog. Her heart stopped as she tried to think of a way to make Duke run.

"No, don't," Kaycee screamed just as a shot rang out, startling her.

The force of the bullet sent Scott flying back, slamming him against the wooden wall of the stall, blood soaking his chest. Kaycee watched as his eyes widened, then slowly grew cold and lifeless.

"Kaycee!"

Turning her head slowly, she saw Sam standing a few feet away. She blinked, unsure she wasn't seeing things as he rushed forward, Tyler close behind him.

"Kaycee," Sam cried as he dropped to the floor next to her. "Tyler, call an ambulance." He lifted her shirt, trying to get a good look at the wound. His breath caught at the gaping hole ripped into her lower stomach. "It's bad, Tyler. Tell them to hurry."

While Tyler called 911, Sam took in Kaycee's injuries. The gash down her leg was long and deep, but it wasn't her most life threatening. The one in her lower stomach was what had him worried, and he removed his shirt, pressing the material against her wound. She whimpered, drawing her legs up against the pain. "Kaycee, baby. Can you hear me?"

"Duke," she whispered.

"He's okay. I promise."

"He tried to save me." Her eyes drifted closed and he shook her. She needed to remain awake.

"Stay with me, Kaycee."

She sobbed, tears streaming down her face. "I can't, Sam. It hurts."

"I know, baby. Just stay with me, okay?"

Gripping her chin, he forced her to meet his gaze. Her eyes were dull, pain-filled, and he'd give anything to trade places with her. "Look at me, baby."

"Tyler?" she sighed.

"I'm here, baby." Tyler dropped to his knees beside her and brushed the hair from her face. "I'm so sorry, Kaycee. We should have never left you alone."

Tyler felt Sam's anguish, his guilt. God, what had they been thinking? They knew he was out there. Her eyes began to flutter closed and all the color drained from her flesh.

"Did you get him?" she asked.

Tyler frowned toward Sam. She'd seen them shoot him.

"Yes, baby," Sam whispered. "We got him. But you've got to stay with me."

Her limbs began to shake and her eyes rolled back in her head. His heart raced in his chest as he tapped her cheek in light slaps, trying to wake her again. "Kaycee, stay with me!"

"Shit, she's going into shock," Tyler growled.

* * *

Sam paced in the waiting room of the hospital, anxiety eating a hole in his stomach. He had no idea how long she'd been in surgery, but the wait was killing him. Glancing toward the other end of the room, he spotted his brother sitting in one of the chairs, head in his hands.

God, what the hell had they been thinking? They weren't trained for the kind of protection she'd needed. Tyler had wanted to bring her to the ranch because of what he'd felt for her. And deep down Sam was glad they had. They'd finally found their one, but they'd almost lost her in the process. They could still lose her. Not from her injuries -- they'd gotten her to the hospital in time -- but because of her own fears. They hadn't told her they loved her. They hadn't wanted to rush her. Now...now all he wanted to do was hold her and tell her they loved her, never let her go. But the decision would have to be hers and hers alone.

The door to the room opened and the surgeon they'd left Kaycee's care to stepped into the room. "Mr. Warren?" he called.

"Yes," he and Tyler both replied in unison.

He stared, his gaze moving back and forth between the two, then glanced at the chart. "Sam Warren," he said.

"That's me," Sam said as he stepped closer, Tyler right behind him. "How is she?"

"She came through surgery fine. Her leg took sixty-three stitches. It looks worse than it is. I understand she's a model, so I had a plastic surgeon take a look. He did the best he could to close it so it wouldn't scar. The stomach wound was my biggest concern. I'm afraid she lost an ovary and a few feet of intestines."

Sam closed his eyes, his stomach knotting. God, if they'd just been in there with her.

"But her uterus still looks good and her other ovary is fine. Children are still in her future if she so chooses, but I would recommend an appointment with a gynecologist just to confirm what I've said."

Sam nodded.

"She lost a lot of blood, so we gave her a transfusion while in surgery. She should be awake soon, although a bit groggy."

"Can we see her?" Sam asked.

"They're wheeling her to recovery now, so I'll have them come get you as soon as she's settled."

"Thank you."

The doctor nodded then left the room. Sam turned to stare at Tyler who looked as relieved as he felt. "Barreck wants us to come to Washington, finish up the paperwork."

"Barreck can go to hell," Tyler growled.

"Tyler."

"I'm not leaving her."

"We need to give her some space. Let her come to us."

"And if she doesn't?"

Sam knew the fear that coursed through Tyler's veins. He felt it, too. But they had to do this. It had to be her decision.

* * *

Kaycee awoke with a start and glanced around the hospital room. Memories from the last three days came back and she sighed toward the ceiling. God, it was finally over. She missed Tyler and Sam, though. They'd come to see her in recovery, explaining they had last minute FBI stuff to take care of. She understood, really, but she hadn't heard from them since they left, even by phone, and it made her heart break.

Sam had explained she needed time to think, time to make her decision. And truthfully, he was right. She had feelings for them -- heaven help her, for both of them -- Sam with his dominant, arrogant personality and Tyler with his charm and smile. They'd stolen her heart so quickly and shown her passion she had only ever imagined existed.

But could a relationship like they wanted really work? Could she really do it?

"It's about time you woke up."

Kaycee opened her eyes and stared in surprise at her agent, Charlotte, standing at the other side of her room in the midst of all the get well flowers and plants. "When did you get here?"

"Yesterday. And let me tell you, it wasn't easy."

Charlotte strolled over and handed Kaycee yet another card, this one from some actor she barely knew. She placed it on the bedside table and tried to sit up. Pain sliced through her stomach and she winced before finally getting to a comfortable position.

"Do you have any idea how many people want to talk to you right now? If you play this right, you'll get loads of exposure."

Rolling her eyes, Kaycee shifted again, trying to ease some of the discomfort. They'd made her walk earlier, and her leg still ached from the exertion even though it had only been a few feet. The doctor seemed to think another day or two and she'd be walking a mile. Kaycee didn't quite agree.

"I'm really not interested in talking to the press, Charlotte," Kaycee said, adjusting the covers carefully over her stomach. "I just want to forget all of this."

All of it but her protectors. Those two she could never forget, no matter how much she tried. God, she missed them.

"Even Victoria's Secret?" Charlotte said with a grin.

"What?"

"They want to sign you."

Kaycee's stomach flipped. "You can't be serious."

She'd wanted a contract with Victoria's Secret since she'd started modeling. She couldn't believe it had finally come through.

"They want you to come to Paris as soon as you're healed."

"Oh, my God."

Her door opened and Jordan swept in, carrying yet another bundle of flowers. Her room couldn't possibly hold any more. She'd have to get the nurses to start distributing them among some of the patients before too much longer.

"Woman, you sure are popular," Jordan said with a grin as she placed her latest bundle on the nightstand next to the bed. "Especially with those FBI agents that were taking care of you."

Kaycee's heart stopped. "Why do you say that?"

"They've called at least twice a day to check on you."

Then it soared. "They have?"

Jordan's fingers arranged the mums and daisies. "Yep, in the morning and again in the evening, just like clockwork."

Kaycee stared down at her lap. They'd said they wanted to give her time, space. But she needed them more than she needed time. She wished she could see them, talk to them, especially now. Unfortunately, other than the location of the ranch, she didn't know how to get a hold of them.

* * *

Two weeks later

Kaycee stood at the airport, ticket to Paris in hand, her gaze glued to the huge jet outside her window. For days she'd agonized over what she really wanted. She'd wanted this contract for so long. She'd worked for it, paid her dues.

Her leg, for the most part, had healed. Her stomach would carry a scar despite everything they'd done, but Victoria's Secret still wanted her. They could airbrush out the scar in photos. It was everything she'd ever wanted, but something wasn't right.

Turning, she caught a glimpse of a man with broad shoulders in a cowboy hat and jeans. Her stomach jerked and she held her breath. Sam? He looked up and met her gaze. It wasn't Sam and sadness filled her chest, tightening her muscles.

Right then, she knew what was missing -- knew what her heart really wanted. It wasn't contracts with famous lingerie companies. It wasn't tickets to Paris. It was two men with eyes the color of a summer sky and smiles that made her heart race. She wanted long summer days working on the ranch and children to run through the yard and teach to ride horses. She wanted Sam and Tyler.

What the hell was she doing?

She made her decision. She didn't think, she just did it.

Turning, she touched her agent on her sleeve. "Charlotte. We need to talk."

* * *

Sam threw a bale of hay toward the far side of the barn loft, trying not to think about another lonely day without Kaycee. It had been two weeks and they hadn't heard a word from her. He was beginning to think they never would. They'd buried Juan on the far side of the ranch at his family's request. He loved it here and his family thought if he and Tyler didn't mind, he should remain there in death.

He and his brother had readily agreed. They had also paid his widow two years' salary, enabling her to begin anew wherever she wanted. It still hadn't helped to ease his guilt though. He would always blame himself for Juan's death.

"Car coming up the drive," one of the hands yelled and he walked over to the opening to stare out toward the distance.

Squinting against the sun, he watched a deep orange Chevy HHR come barreling up the gravel road and his heart stopped. Kaycee drove an HHR. Was that her? He took off his gloves and threw them onto the pile of hay bales before quickly descending the ladder. He walked out of the barn just as Kaycee pulled to a stop a few feet away from him and climbed from the car.

She stood there wedged between the open car door and the driver's side, watching him almost warily. The cool wind blew her hair around her face, reddening her cheeks. God, she looked good. So much better than the last time he'd seen her at the hospital.

Duke came barreling past Sam toward Kaycee. Her face lit up, her smile spreading across her face like a ray of sunshine.

"Duke," she cried, then laughed when the golden retriever jumped up, placing his paws against her stomach. She ruffled his ears, placing a quick kiss on the end of his nose. "My hero," she cooed, making Sam smile.

With one final pat to his head, she straightened, then turned to face Sam, her eyes expressive and full of uncertainty. "You left me," she said simply, watching him closely.

"I never left you, Kaycee. I just wanted to give you a little space. Tyler and I were asking a lot of you."

He wanted to run to her, kiss her, hold her forever, but he remained rooted to the spot, waiting for her.

"Yes, you are," she replied and his gut clenched. "There are some things we'll need to work out…discuss."

Sam nodded.

"I want a wedding. On the beach in Fiji. And children."

"What?" he whispered, holding his breath.

"Children. At least two. One from you and one from Tyler. I talked to Charlotte. She let me out of my contract early and --"

Sam didn't give her a chance to finish. He stomped forward, pulled her from behind the door, and wrapped his arms around her, practically bending her backward as his mouth devoured hers. She laughed into his kiss, her arms rising to hold tightly to his neck. She was willing to give it a try. Every part of him wanted to jump for joy like a kid, scream at the world that she was his -- his and his brother's.

"I love you," he said as he smiled against her lips.

"I almost went to Paris, Sam." She shook her head, blinking back tears. "But I saw this man at the airport and realized I wanted you and Tyler more."

"You won't regret leaving modeling?" he asked.

"No. No way."

"Hey! What about me?"

They both turned to look at Tyler, who stood to the side watching them with a wide grin spreading across his face. With a squeal, Kaycee left Sam's arms and flew into Tyler's. His brother laughed.

"I love you, Tyler. Both of you."

"Not near as much as I love you," Tyler teased as he pulled back to really look at her. "How are you, baby? Are you okay?"

She nodded.

"She informed me she wants kids," Sam said with a grin. "One mine, one yours."

Tyler smiled. "Kids, huh? I think we can handle that."

"I think the first thing we should do is plan a trip to Amarillo," Sam said. Kaycee turned to look at him and he smiled. "Mom's gonna want to meet you and I'm dying to see my father bowing in awe."

Kaycee's laughter surrounded them. Sam laughed as well, his chest expanding with so much love and happiness he thought he'd explode. His mother had been right all those years ago. There really was a woman out there made for them and she was right here -- right where she belonged.

Epilogue

Five years later

"Good morning, Mrs. Warren."

Kaycee looked up and smiled at the bank teller, an older lady by the name of Mary. It had taken her a while to get used to small-town life. Everyone here knew everyone, and she'd been shocked to discover most of the town knew about Sam and Tyler and the fact she was married to both of them. To her surprise, they'd accepted her with open arms, welcoming her as though she'd been there all her life.

"When's that baby due?"

With a smile, Kaycee put her hand on her huge stomach. "Any day now."

Despite the doctor's assurance she could have children, it had taken several months for her to get pregnant. When she finally had, they'd all cried.

"Do you know the sex yet?"

She nodded. "Yep. One boy and one girl."

The teller's eyes widened and her lips lifted into a happy smile. "Twins? Why that's wonderful! Sam and Tyler must be just thrilled."

With a grin, Kaycee leaned forward. "Between you and me, they're scared to death."

They both giggled.

"Men are always scared to death," Mary said with a wave of her hand. "They're smart men. They'll learn fast."

Kaycee smiled, thinking about both her husbands searching the Internet for baby furniture and toys. They'd planned to do it right, so they would know who fathered each child, but it hadn't worked out that way. She had no idea which one had fathered the twins and since Sam and Tyler were identical, they would never know. They would each show as a possible father in a DNA test.

But the men didn't care, or at least didn't seem to. They were both just as excited as the other, both just as determined to be the best father they could be. If they showed these children the same love they showed her, they would be lucky children indeed.

With a smile, she told Mary good-bye and left the bank, anxious to get home to her husbands. She never once regretted her decision to leave modeling. She had no doubt she was right where she belonged.

THE END

Trista Ann Michaels

Trista lives in the land of dreams, where alpha men are tender and heroines are strong and sassy. When not there, she visits the mountains of Tennessee. Not a bad place to spend a little spare time when she needs a break from all those voices in her head. Unfortunately they never fail to find her.

TITLES AVAILABLE In Print from Loose Id®

ALPHA
Treva Harte

COURTESAN
Louisa Trent

DANGEROUS CRAVINGS
Evangeline Anderson

DAUGHTERS OF TERRA:
THE TA'E'SHA CHRONICLES, BOOK ONE
Theolyn Boese

DINAH'S DARK DESIRE
Mechele Armstrong

FORGOTTEN SONG
Ally Blue

HARD CANDY
Angela Knight, Morgan Hawke and Sheri Gilmore

HEAVEN SENT: HELL & PURGATORY
Jet Mykles

HEAVEN SENT 2
Jet Mykles

HOWL
Jet Mykles, Raine Weaver, and Jeigh Lynn

INTERSTELLAR SERVICE & DISCIPLINE:
VICTORIOUS STAR
Morgan Hawke

LEASHED: MORE THAN A BARGAIN
Jet Mykles

ROMANCE AT THE EDGE: In Other Worlds
MaryJanice Davidson, Angela Knight and Camille Anthony

SHARDS OF THE MIND:
THE TA'E'SHA CHRONICLES, BOOK TWO
Theolyn Boese

SLAVE BOY
Evangeline Anderson

STRENGTH IN NUMBERS
Rachel Bo

THEIR ONE AND ONLY
Trista Ann Michaels

THE BITE BEFORE CHRISTMAS
Laura Baumbach, Sedonia Guillone, and Kit Tunstall

THE BROKEN H
J. L. Langley

THE COMPLETENESS OF CELIA FLYNN
Sedonia Guillone

THE PRENDARIAN CHRONICLES
Doreen DeSalvo

THE TIN STAR
J. L. Langley

WHY ME?
Treva Harte

WILD WISHES
Stephanie Burke, Lena Matthews, and Eve Vaughn

Publisher's Note: The print titles listed above were previously released in e-book format by Loose Id®.

Non-Fiction by **ANGELA KNIGHT**
PASSIONATE INK: A GUIDE TO WRITING EROTIC ROMANCE

Printed in the United States
134991LV00001B/131/P

9 781596 327535